The Golden Seal

JAMES VANCE MARSHALL

The Golden Seal

Illustrated by Maurice Wilson

DRAGON
Granada Publishing

Dragon Books
Granada Publishing Ltd
8 Grafton Street, London W1X 3LA

Published by Dragon Books 1984
First published as *A River Ran Out of Eden*
by Hodder and Stoughton Ltd in 1962

Copyright © Donald Payne 1962

ISBN 0-583-30719-1

Printed and bound in Great Britain by
Hazell Watson & Viney Limited,
Aylesbury, Bucks

'If a man offend a harmless, pure and innocent person, the evil falls back upon that fool, like light dust thrown up against the wind.'

The Dhammapada of Buddha IX 9

Author's Note

I first heard of the golden seal fifty years ago when, as a deck-hand in the *Fusan Maru*, I spent a season trading in pelts and walrus tusks among the Aleutian Islands. Zoologists will assure you no such animal exists. Believers in Aleut folk lore will assure you it does. I don't presume to judge.

J. V. M.

I

THE Great Bank lies along the southern shore of Unimak, an island close to the tip of Alaska. It is one of the most remote and lonely places in the world: a twenty-mile ribbon of shingle and sand-dune which rises, falls and breathes to the recurrent beat of waves and tide. For years no one set foot on it; for behind it lay a virgin island, its secrets unexplored, and in front of it a tangled skein of reefs and sandbars—a race of water too troubled for the sealers and fisherfolk of Dutch Harbour to risk their boats in.

Greys and yellows and gentle greens are the colours of the bank, colours which are most of the time muted by mist, like those of a faded water-colour. But sometimes, at sunrise or sunset, land and sea and sky will catch fire, and the pinions of the wild geese and cormorants as they fly to their nesting ground among the sandhills will be tipped with vermilion and gold.

Close to the western extremity of the bank a little river flows out through the sandhills and into the sea. Its waters are crystal clear, being fed by the snows of Shishaldin (Unimak's 9,000-foot volcano), its pools at spawn time seethe with salmon, and its banks in spring and early summer are

gay with a tangle of lemon rhododendrons. In most places the rhododendrons grow thickly, clothing either bank in a mosaic of reseda and gold; but at the place where the river makes its final turn before entering the sea, the bushes are unexpectedly sparse. Come close and you will see why. There, blackened with age, are the unmistakable cuts of axe and billhook; there a half-filled depression where a stump has been grubbed laboriously out of the sand; and there a litter of rhododendron limbs which someone, long ago, tossed carelessly into a random pile. Come closer still and you will see something else: built into the bank a hexagonal concrete pillbox-cum-radar-post, half buried in the sand like the carcass of some strange monster from another world. Its slit eyes are sealed with sea kelp now; its walls are crumbling and cracked; the cracks are green with salt and verdigris; and the rhododendrons are beginning to close round it, to claim back their own.

Many years ago this pillbox served a useful purpose, giving radar warning of possible Japanese air attacks on the Alcan Highway. But the tide of war ebbed past the Aleutians, the usefulness of the post came to an end, the Marines who manned it were withdrawn and it fell into disrepair. For years no one remembered it was there.

But lately it came to serve again as a human habitation. To it there came a man and a woman: a grey-haired sealer, big boned and slow moving, and his bride, a young Aleut girl with slant blue eyes and a voice as soft as the snow of Shishaldin. They were Unimak's sole inhabitants.

It is about them, their children and the man whose path for a few brief days crossed theirs that this story is told. It is not a story that falls smoothly and easily into sequence. For things that look simple on the surface have a habit, when probed into, of turning out to be unexpectedly complex; and of the principal actors one lies buried beneath the foothills of Shishaldin, one is a child whose innocence too probing a questioning might destroy, and the wild and beautiful creature with the gold-tipped fur which was the cause of it all has vanished beneath the grey Aleutian waves.

2

IT was in the late spring of 1952 that Jim and Tania Lee came to Unimak.

Jim Lee had spent nearly all his forty-seven years trapping, fishing and sealing in and around the Aleutians. Most men in his calling work for a company—either the Northern Fur Corporation or one of the firms of salmon-canners whose offices line the quay at Dutch Harbour. But Jim Lee worked for himself. He owned a two-masted ten-and-a-half ton yawl, the *Bear* (with the R on the stern painted Russian-wise, back-to-front), which he sailed alone among the mist-wreathed islands with wonderful skill. Several companies had offered him tempting terms to join them—for few men were his equal at handling boat, trap or harpoon. But Jim Lee preferred to remain his own master. One of his reasons could be seen at a glance. The left-hand side of his face was disfigured. From temple to jaw ran a livid bone-deep scar, a relic of the Japanese reign of co-prosperity on Okinawa. The scar wasn't a pretty sight and Jim Lee knew it. Disliking sympathy, he had come gradually to prefer his own company to that of others.

Tania was a few weeks past her eighteenth birthday when Jim took her from a Dutch Harbour brothel, married her in the red-roofed, green-domed Church of Saint Peter, and brought her—for reasons of his own—to Unimak. She was taller and slimmer than the average Aleut and far prettier; but the olive gloss of her skin and the Mongolian slant of her eyes stamped her, unmistakably, for what she was: a squaw. Jim's friends were surprised when he married her; it was, they felt, one thing to shack-up with a squaw for two or three months; but to get saddled with one for life . . .! They were even more surprised when Jim and the girl set off for Unimak, an uninhabited island 150 miles from Dutch Harbour. The men of the world all shook their heads at this; they'll be back in a twelve-month, they said; or at least *she* will be.

But the men of the world were wrong.

Jim and Tania built their *barabara* on the foundations of the abandoned pillbox. Beside the house they built a *beleek* hut for smoking salmon and a sod cabin for storing pelts. Then they settled down to a life of primeval simplicity.

The island was theirs and all that was in it; the beasts of tundra and grassland, the fish of river and sea and the birds of the Great Bank—the wild geese, cormorants and gulls which nested in their tens of thousands among the sand-dunes and sedge grass.

In winter they trapped blue and arctic fox on the fringe of Shishaldin's snow line. In summer they shot snowshoe rabbits and Kodiak bears. At spawn time they hauled in their wicker-work traps seething with salmon which they split, hung on willow frames and smoked in the *beleek* hut over a fire of driftwood and straw. They set long-lines among the off-shore shoals. They set trap-lines by moonlight on slopes of virgin snow. They made love and raised children and were happy as Adam and Eve before the Fall. And in between times they searched for the semi-legendary golden seals—'they with the yellow hair' the Aleuts called them—which are among the rarest and most beautiful of all created creatures.

It was because of the golden seals that Jim had come to Unimak.

'They with the yellow hair' are thought to be a rare mutation of the Pacific Seals which summer and breed in the Prebilov Islands. They are creatures of solitude. They spend their lives far out at sea, among the mid-ocean patches of kelp. Only very occasionally are they driven ashore by storm; and it is then, as they crawl battered and exhausted on to the rocks, that they are sometimes shot by the sealers. Sometimes but not often. For in Jim's forty-odd years in the Aleutians less than a dozen golden pelts had ever been brought into Dutch Harbour. They fetched 2,000 dollars apiece.

Jim was determined to have one. It wasn't so much the 2,000 dollars that fired his imagination—though that to a sealer was Eldorado—it was the challenge to his prowess as a hunter. Over the years he made a study of all that was known of the golden seals and he unearthed one fact which interested him greatly. Of the dozen pelts brought to Dutch Harbour over half had been shot off Unimak, where the prevailing currents and storm tracks sometimes drove the gold-furred seals on to the tail of the Great Bank. After he had made this discovery Jim spent much time sailing the *Bear* in and out of Unimak's reefs and sand-bars. He saw his quarry twice, but neither time was he close enough to get in a shot; and eventually he decided to land on Unimak, to build himself a temporary home close to the tail of the bank.

And so the *barabara* came to be built, and the foxes trapped and the salmon smoked and the sea-fowl snared, and whenever they had time to spare Jim and Tania tramped the gravel and sand-dune strand, searching.

To Jim's disappointment they found no golden seal. But as the years passed they found, in a gradual accidental sort of way, something else: complete and utter happiness. They had their island and they had each other and they wanted nothing more. Nor was their happiness a transient thing,

14

born only of novelty and physical passion. As the years passed, it deepened and matured in a way that sometimes made both of them almost a little afraid: afraid that such happiness as theirs was too perfect to last, was like a full-blown rose, too beautiful to see the sun-up of another day.

By the summer of 1960 they had been on the Great Bank eight years—eight years of Arcadian idyll broken only by some dozen trips to Dutch Harbour to buy stores and sell their pelts. And in those eight years the only thing to cloud their happiness was the fact that they found no golden seal.

This troubled Jim more than Tania. He continued to spend a great deal of time tramping the sand-dunes, his dream unfulfilled. He even built a series of sod huts along the bank so that he could keep watch in time of storm. And as the years passed the killing of a golden seal became a sort of millennium to him, a panacea for every ill. They wanted a transmitting set, an outboard motor, a new stove? They'd have them as soon as he shot the golden seal. Such were the concrete reasons for his carrying on with the search. But there was another reason too. Pride. Jim Lee valued his reputation as a hunter. How greatly that reputation would be enhanced when he sailed in triumph into Dutch Harbour with the pelt of one of the semi-legendary golden seals! In his dreams he sometimes saw himself striding into the Cornucopia, slinging the pelt on to the bar and calling for drinks for the house, and in his dream the men who had shunned him because of his scar and the men who had looked down their noses at him because of his squaw would drink his health and sing his praise; 'So that,' they would say, 'is why you buried yourself on Unimak'; and their voices would be admiring.

But Tania didn't share his enthusiasm.

She, to tell the truth, was almost glad that no golden seal was found. It was as if she knew, intuitively, that the finding of one would lead to complication and change.

3

THE summer of 1960 was unusually warm and dry in the
Aleutians. All through July and August Unimak lay
like a mirage, a mist-wreathed island asleep in a mercury
sea. Shishaldin's snow line receded, the river shrank, the
rhododendrons wilted and died and cast-up medusas strewed
the bank, their blood-red veins—like the spokes of a Japanese flag—melting on the sun-hot stones.

Such a heat wave, Jim Lee knew, could have only one
end: a summer storm. And summer storms in the Aleutians
are suddener and wickeder than anywhere else on earth;
those caught in the open in them die.

Early in the morning of August 30th Jim Lee climbed the
sandhills at the back of the *barabara*. He reached the crest and
stood looking about him, silhouetted by the rays of the
rising sun.

Beneath him the Great Bank lay like a sleeping child,
motionless and beautiful in the pale half-light of dawn. No
wave whispered over the surface of a sea of glass; no breath
of wind disturbed the drooping leaves of the rhododendrons;
at the water's edge the sea-fowl huddled in little groups,
still as stage-props; and beside the river three little Kodiak
bears squatted like patient old-men anglers watching
the salmon. Jim Lee surveyed his kingdom, and was
content.

But suddenly his eyes, following the sweep of the shore,
narrowed. He stared, grunted and walked down to the edge
of the sea.

He looked at the unfamiliar scumline, at the froth of fine almost transparent tendrils of vegetation cast up by the tide. He knew what the vegetation was. Sea kelp. And he knew its cause. Somewhere away in the south a great hurricane was walking the Pacific: a hurricane so violent that its underwater waves were wrenching the tangled kelp off the bed of the sea, churning it to the surface and driving it in front of them like the *tirailleurs* of an advancing host.

He looked at the sky and it was blue and innocent; he looked at the sea and it was serene as the eyes of a nun. But he wasn't deceived. He knew that somewhere beyond the horizon the hurricane was lurking: dangerous, unpredictable; and he shivered, touched by a sudden unease. He tried to shrug it aside; he told himself that Unimak had been in the path of storms before—and they'd survived. But the unease refused to leave him. Thoughtfully he walked back to the *barabara*.

He got the children—Eric aged seven and Jess aged three —to help him slot wooden shutters into the window frames; he got Tania to help him haul in and lash down the *Bear*. Together they checked the foundation sods round the base of the pillbox, doubled the guy-wires holding down the roof and brought in supplies of water and food. And he told the children not to go out of sight of the house.

All day they waited for the storm to break. But all day the sky remained cloudless; there wasn't a breath of wind, and Shishaldin's snow spire, upside down, lay mirrored in a sea of glass. Come sundown and a breathlessness of mist came creeping in from the sea. It was so still and airless that it was difficult to sleep. The children were fretful and Tania frightened—a storm to an Aleut is not just a natural phenomenon but a manifestation of the wrath of the gods—and all night she sat by the open door watching the close-packed tendrils of brown come drifting in with the tide.

By next morning the sea kelp had thickened; had thick-

ened to such an extent that it blotted out the sea. There was no water left now to mirror Shishaldin's spire. From shore to horizon the sea wrack stretched in a vast unbroken sheet: silent as sleep, motionless as death.

Tania looked at it and reached for Jim's hand. He squeezed hers reassuringly at the same time turning his head so that she shouldn't see him moisten his lips. Never in all his years in the Aleutians had he known the sea like this: throttled to a stillness so absolute it could almost be felt.

After breakfast he suggested that the whole family set-to to haul in the salmon traps—the last time there was a storm the river had flooded and three of their traps had been swept out to sea. The idea pleased everyone except Eric. The little boy had helped himself to his father's binoculars (which he had just learned to focus) and he was sitting at the side of the *barabara* methodically scannir g the sea kelp. At his parents' approach he jumped up.

'Can I have your glasses, Dad?'

'Looks like you got 'em!'

'But can I keep 'em?'

'You can bring 'em along to the traps if you like.'

His face fell. 'But I don't want to come to the traps. I want to stay here, watchin' the kelp.'

Jim shook his head. 'Tell you what, Eric. You give us a hand with the traps. Soon as they're all in, you an' me'll go to the top of the bank and watch the kelp from there. O.K?'

'All right then'—reluctantly—'long as we aren't too long.'

They headed up-river. Eric had left the binoculars behind; he didn't mention the sea kelp again until just before they came to the traps. Then he tugged at his father's sleeve.

'Dad!'

'Yes?'

'It's true, isn't it, that golden seals live in kelp?'

Jim Lee nodded. So that's what the boy had been looking for. And it was quite an idea too . . .

It was less than five minutes walk up-river to where the traps were slung like great wickerwork cocoons from bank to bank. They were easy to haul in. Jim and Tania waded into the water and methodically loosened the ropes and pulled the baskets into the shallows. To start with Eric helped them, but after a while he got bored and hoisted himself on to the bank. For some minutes he snapped off rhododendron twigs, tossed them into the water and raced them down-river; but that too failed to hold his attention for long. He was restless. Eventually he sidled up to his father.

'Dad! Can I go home?'

'What you want to go home for?'

'I got a headache.'

Jim and Tania looked at each other. 'It's sure headache weather,' she said.

Jim hesitated. Had the boy really a headache? Or did he just want to get back to the *barabara* to watch the kelp? And what if he did? He could hardly come to any harm.

'All right then. But straight back, you hear.'

'Thanks, Dad.'

'Now listen to me, Eric. This is important. Because there's going to be a storm soon. Promise you'll go straight home. And promise you'll not go out of sight of the house.'

'Cross my heart.'

And the little boy, swishing at the dried-up leaves with his rhododendron branch, set off down-river.

It would, Jim told himself, take him less than five minutes to get back to the *barabara*. And he had taught the children never to break a promise.

Even in the water it was hot and airless. And quiet too. In the oppressive silence the splatter of water as Jim and Tania hauled in the traps sounded loud as the cascade of a waterfall. The traps came in easily. For they were empty. The salmon had buried themselves deep in the mud. Nor was it only the fish which had disappeared. After a while Jim noticed that the bank, like the river, was devoid of life. The sea-fowl had vanished. Even the frightless gulls had fled the path of the storm.

He looked at the sky. The mist had cleared now, and the southern horizon was hard and curiously bright. He kept his voice casual.

'Guess we'd best be headin' back.'

They hauled the traps to the top of the bank and tossed them well out of reach of the water. Then they picked up Jess and headed for home.

Jim's casualness didn't deceive Tania. 'Jim! Something's going to happen.'

'Nothin' but a storm.'

'Something else. I know.'

She was trembling and staring this way and that like a trapped animal.

His hand closed over hers.

'It's a natural thing, Tania. Jest wind and rain and big waves. It'll all be over in twenty-four hours.'

A sudden breath of wind whispered among the sedge grass and scuffed up the shrivelled leaves. He let go her hand and hoisted Jess high on his shoulder.

'Let's go.'

A couple of minutes heading down-stream and they could see ahead of them the sheet of the sea kelp, lacquered to shininess by the heat of the sun. Something was happening to it. They stopped and stared, amazed. For the kelp was undulating rhythmically: was rising and falling to the swell of under-surface waves. Even as they watched, it split: cracked open with a series of sharp reports like the rattle of far-off small-arms; a wide-spaced swell came surging up to the shore, and rollers, curiously loud, began to pound at the bank.

Jim tucked his daughter under his arm.

'Quick! Run!'

And they rushed for the *barabara*.

They were half-way there when the light went out of the day. From behind the spire of Shishaldin a great copper cloud poured like discoloured ink across the sky. The sun was swallowed up. A dull ochre light enveloped the island, and a wayward wind hot and wet as a sirocco began to slam this way and that in random gusts. As they neared the *barabara*, sea drift and ripped-off fragments of kelp came scudding in from the sea.

'Eric!' Tania's call was frightened. 'Eric! Eric!'

There was no reply.

Beside the door a hurricane lantern swung from the rafters. Jim's hands as he lit it were trembling. Light flooded the *barabara*, spotlighting the table in the centre of the room, throwing into sharp relief the sheet of paper kept in position on the wooden boards with one of Jim Lee's sea boots.

'Dear Dad,

I am goin to loke for a gold seal. I will take care of your glases.

Yours sinserly,
Eric

I did come strate home and where I am going I can see home with the glases from.'

Tania covered her face. She rocked to and fro.

'Oh no!' Her voice was a whisper. 'Oh no. No. No. No.'

Then with a wild low-pitched moan the storm was on them.

4

THE lantern swung wildly. A tinkle of glass. Darkness. A second of shocked silence. Then under a hammer-blow of wind the door burst open, a chair picked up like a straw, cartwheeled across the room, a shutter splintered against its frame and Jess screamed—a high-pitched scream of terror. Tania rushed to her and bundled her into her cot. Jim flung himself at the door—he needed all his strength to force it shut. Then he struggled with the shutters, battening them down against the malevolent tug and wrench of an eighty-knot wind. Behind him Tania struck match after match, but not till the last shutter was fast did a flame burn long enough to catch the wick of the safety lamp. Then a frightened glimmer of light crept round the *barabara*.

'Eric!' Tania rocked to and fro, her hands to her eyes.

'Listen.' Jim gripped her by the shoulder. 'He'll be all right. He's a sensible boy. He'll go to one of the sod huts.'

'Perhaps he'll try to get back.'

The moan of the storm swelled to a high-pitched shriek. A hail of gravel, ripped off the face of the bank, pitted into the walls of the hut and the whole building quivered and shook like a ship whose rivets were loosening under the pound of a mighty sea. Jim knew that if his son hadn't found shelter there was nothing that he or anyone else could do to save him. But he knew too that he had to try.

They up-ended the table and pushed it against Jess's cot (to protect her from flung-in stones); they dragged up a heavy chair (to jam open the door), and Jim tied a length of rope round his waist and tossed the end to Tania.

'If I'm in trouble I'll jerk the rope. And you haul me in.'

He wedged the chair at an angle under the crosspiece of the door. He drew back the bolt. The door flung open. A torrent of wind, spindrift, gravel and sand poured flood-like into the *barabara*. And he crawled out, on hands and knees, into the storm.

Tania's knuckles were in her mouth. Her teeth were clenched, and blood ran warm through her fingers.

'Don't go. Oh please don't go.'

But her voice was lost in the wind and he was gone and she was alone with the slack of the rope.

It was another world he crawled into, a world which in the space of a couple of minutes had lost its normal division into land and sea and sky and had shrunk to one wild kaleido-scopic mêlée in which cloud and rain and spume and gravel and sand were merged into one frenetic whirlwind blown screaming off the face of the earth. As he edged out from behind the doorway, the wind struck him like a physical blow. It knocked him flat. It sucked the breath out of his lungs. For a full minute he lay spread-eagled, gasping and retching. Then he began to worm his way to the end of the *barabara*. Shielding his eyes, he peered at the bank: at the cluster of sand-dunes Eric was most likely to have climbed. But everything was dark and blurred and shifting as the wind ripped off sand and stone, now from one crest now from another, and flung it hither and thither like chaff from a gargantuan thresher. Of his son there was no sign. He peered seaward trying to get his bearings. Down on the shore he thought he saw something he could hardly credit, some-thing that looked like a boat, a dismasted dory, broached-to and battered by the great waves. Was it really a boat? Or was it some strange hallucination of the storm? He couldn't be sure. But in any case it wasn't his son. He turned to the bank. He tried to scan it methodically, section by section. But by now the hammer-blows of wind had sapped his strength and bludgeoned him to a punch-drunk daze. His eyes refused to focus. He didn't see the sky ahead turn suddenly black. Before he knew what was happening the flying gravel hit him, smashing like hail into an arm flung instinctively over his face. He was toppled head over heels to the foot of the dunes.

He lay on his stomach, his bruised hands clawing at the sand, the waves of pain like excited cymbals crashing *accelerando* inside his brain. He tried to get to his knees, but the bank toppled sideways and the sand slipped out from beneath him and he knew he was going to faint. His hands dropped, and as they dropped one of them brushed the rope. The last thing he remembered was the pain of his hands, tightening and jerking, again and again and again. Then silence and a long, long merciful slide into the dark.

Tania was sheltering behind the half-open door when the rope jerked.

She licked her lips. She tried to peer out, but the flying gravel forced her back. She braced her feet against the doorpost and hauled on the rope. It came in reluctantly, dead weight. She went on hauling, hand over hand, until at last she saw him: limp as a puppet, face down in the sand. She pulled her anorak over her head and squirmed out of the doorway.

'Oh Jim!' she whispered. She whispered it over and over again. 'Oh Jim! Oh Jim! Oh Jim!'

And she took him under the armpits and dragged him inch by painful inch into the shelter of the *barabara*.

She hadn't the weight to shut the door; she had to lever it to with a crowbar. She fetched a sponge and a bowl of water. She was bathing the dirt and blood away from his face and hands when his eyes flickered open. He tried to smile at her.

'Don't worry.' His voice was broken as his hands. 'He's not outside. He must be in one of the sod huts.'

'I know. Don't talk.'

And she went on sponging the dirt, very gently, away from his face.

They sat on the floor of the *barabara* and sipped mugs of cocoa and listened to the noise of the storm. There was nothing else they could do.

They didn't talk much: for all there was to say could be said in a dozen words. If Eric had found shelter he was safe; if he hadn't he was dead. That was the fact of it, and talk could make it neither better nor worse.

Jim, his hands bandaged and the scar on his face throbbing like the nerve of a tooth, was glad to lie quiet. But Tania was restless. She heated pan after pan of cocoa; she trimmed and re-trimmed the lamps; she checked and re-checked the shutters; she paced the *barabara*, distraught, starting and trembling at every new note in the storm's cacophony; up and down, down and up, round and round her foot-falls

26

pattered like the beat of pinioned wings. Suddenly she stood very still. Her eyes were frightened.

'Jim. Don't ever change.'

'Change? Why should I?'

'Please promise me you'll never change.'

He sensed her urgency.

'All right. I promise.'

Some of the fear ebbed out of her. She sat beside him.

'I'm frightened, Jim. We've been too happy. The gods are jealous. Now they're trying to destroy us.'

He started to remonstrate, but she sprang up, her hand to her mouth.

'What's that?'

The wind bludgeoned the hut. The shingle beat against the walls. And there was another sound as well: a faint insistent sound, a scratching and scrabbling at the *barabara* door. A pause. A dull thud. And the latch jerked uncertainly.

Tania's eyes widened in terror.

Another thud. Another jerk on the latch.

'Eric?' Jim's voice was incredulous. He swung off the bed. Tania grabbed him.

'No!' Her voice started as a whisper and ended as a scream. 'No! It's not Eric. It's the devil. Don't let him in.'

He pushed her aside. He swung his bandaged hand at the bolt. The door flew open. And a man, his face and arms covered in blood, was flung by the wind into the *barabara*. Arms and legs aflail like a rag doll he spun across the threshold, pitched face down at Tania's feet and lay still.

5

THE little boy had no difficulty in fording the river; the water was barely up to his ankles. Then, with many a backward glance to be sure he was keeping the *barabara* in sight, he started up the bank. In one hand were his father's binoculars, in the other a rhododendron branch with which he flicked the melting medusas out of his path. In twenty minutes he was on top of the highest sand-dune.

The view was magnificent. Behind him the river snaking the slopes of Shishaldin; to his left the estuary, with the *barabara* a pinpoint on its farther shore (it was still in sight if he got it in the viewfinder of the binoculars, so he hadn't *really* broken his promise); and in front of him the vast expanse of sea kelp, unbroken and brown as a salmon berry. He focused the glasses on it.

He couldn't make out at first what was wrong; couldn't understand why, in the viewfinder of the binoculars, the image of the kelp kept on blurring and slipping out of focus. It seemed to be moving. It was several minutes before he realized it really *was* moving, was undulating up and down in wide-spaced rhythmic swells. Eric was fascinated. He lay face down on the stones, legs wide apart, glasses riveted on the moving mosaic of kelp. All else was forgotten; golden seals, parents, storm; he was rapt in his discovery, lost to the world. He didn't see the great copper-coloured cloud flooding out against the wind from behind the spire of Shishaldin, he didn't see the stir of the sedge grass in the hot sirocco wind. Only when the sea kelp split and the spume came scudding inland and the waves began to pound the shore did he realize something was wrong.

He jumped up. He spun round. He saw the great cloud swallowing the sky. In terror he stood irresolute, like a sea-bird poised for flight, a wind-torn papier-mâché silhouette dwarfed by the immensity of sea and cloud. Then he began to run.

Nine boys out of ten (nine hundred and ninety-nine town-bred boys out of a thousand) would have run for home, for the reassuring arms of their parents. But Eric ran for the sod hut, for the nearest of the dozen or so shelters built along the crest of the bank. That was the lesson his father had always drummed into him: 'If you're out in a storm take shelter at once; never get caught in the open.' The sod hut was nearer than the *barabara* and so he ran for the sod hut.

He ran for his life, his feet sinking and slipping on the loose-packed stones, while about him the sky grew darker, the wind stronger and the bank began to tremble to the pound of steepening waves. At last his goal was in sight

—the squat mound of turves sunk igloo-like into the ground. He was within a hundred yards of it when the light went suddenly out of the sky. A gust of wind knocked him off his feet. He didn't get up. He shook his head and crawled on. Beneath him the stones began to shift, and loose sand to stream in tattered pennants off the crests of the sand-dunes. He kept his face close to the gravel and crawled on. It seemed a very long way to the shelter. After a while he began to doubt if he'd have the strength to reach it; but at last his fingers were clawing at the circle of sods.

He collapsed face down on the threshold, gasping for breath. And the first thing he noticed was the smell. For a second he drew back, uncertain. Then the gravel beat stinging against his legs, and he squirmed quickly in.

The sod hut was small and dark; it had no window or chimney; its door was simply a couple of movable turves which Eric, from the inside, now hauled-to to keep out the wind. As the turves were pulled in the moan of the storm faded, the last glimmer of light was snuffed out, and the smell—strong and foetid—rose pungently out of the dark. On the far side of the sod hut something moved.

The little boy peered into the darkness, suddenly afraid.

Twin orbs of fire swayed up from the floor: twin balls of red aglow like oriflammes in the dark. And Eric shrank back, appalled. Something was in the sod hut: some wild and terrible animal—perhaps a great Kodiak bear with foot-long claws that could rip the guts from a caribou in a single slash. He spun round. He tore at the door turves. Then he remembered the storm.

He stood very still, teeth clenched, eyes screwed tight. Waiting. But the wild and terrible animal didn't spring at him. Everything was motionless and very quiet—everything except his heart which was pounding in frightened leaps between mouth and stomach, and after a while even the pound of his heart sank to a muffled uncertain throb.

Hesitantly he unscrewed his eyes, ready to snap them shut the moment the animal moved. But the orbs of red were motionless. The creature—whatever it was—kept to the farther side of the hut.

He peered into the blackness. At first he could see only the red of the eyes, but gradually as he became accustomed to the dark he could make out more: a shadowy mass, coiled and menacing, stretching almost a third of the way round the wall. The animal was large; but—to his unspeakable relief—it wasn't thickset and solid enough to be a bear. He began to breathe more easily.

After a while he became conscious of a faint persistent sound: a sound so low that it had been drowned up to now by the thud of his heart and the background moan of the storm. It was a sucky, slobbery sound: a sound he had heard before —years and years ago when he was very small; it wasn't a sound to be frightened of; he knew that; its associations were pleasant. His fear ebbed a little. Perhaps the creature was friendly; perhaps it would let him stay; perhaps the hut was a refuge they could both, in time of emergency, share.

His mind seized on to the idea, thankfully. He remembered a picture in one of his story books: a picture of a little boy (no older than he was) and all sorts of different animals lying together on a flood-ringed island; and he remembered his father reading the caption, 'Then the wolf shall dwell with the lamb, and the leopard shall lie down with the bird, and the young lion and the fatling together,' and he remembered his father explaining that in times of great danger— fire or flood, tempest or drought—all living things reverted to their natural (sinless) state and lived peacefully together until the danger was passed. This, he told himself, must be such a time.

He stared at the glowing eyes. And quite suddenly his fear was submerged in a great flood of curiosity. What *was* this strange red-eyed creature? It was too big for a fox or a hare, and not the right shape for a bear or a caribou. If only he could see it!

He remembered then that somewhere in every sod hut his father had cached matches and candles.

An older boy would have hesitated now. An older boy would have had second thoughts and a legacy of fear. But to Eric things were uncomplicated. He *had* been frightened, but that was in the past: *now* he was curious. For a little boy of seven it was as simple as that.

He felt round the wall till his hand struck a metal box. He prized off the lid. He found and lit one of the candles. A flickering light leapt round the hut. And the little boy's breath stuck in his throat and he could only stare and stare. For never in all his life had he seen anything so beautiful.

She lay curled up against the wall: a sinuous seven-foot golden seal, her fur like a field of sun-drenched corn; and clinging to her teats two soft-furred pups, their eyes still closed.

'Ooooh!' he whispered.

Holding the candle high, his fear quite lost in wonder, he walked towards her.

'Ooooh!' he whispered. 'You're beautiful. An' your babies.'

One of the pups, frightened by his voice, fell away from its mother and went snuffling round the floor. He bent down to pick it up.

The golden seal drew in her head. Her lips writhed back. Her eyes turned suddenly dark.

'It's all right,' the little boy said softly, 'you needn't be scared. I know what to do.'

And very gently he picked up the pup and clamped it back on its teat.

A hint of hesitation or fear and she would have killed him. But his assurance took her aback; her head swayed this way and that like a cobra's, but she didn't strike.

He looked at her brightly. 'I bet you're hungry. Let's find something to eat.'

And he turned his back on her and started to forage inside the tin.

In it he found all manner of intriguing things; bandages, blocks of solid fuel and food—bars of chocolate and cuts of *beleek*-smoked salmon. He didn't know how to use the fuel, but the food he sorted into two piles.

'The chocolate's for me,' he told the golden seal. 'The salmon's for you.'

She looked at him balefully. When he pushed the food towards her she didn't touch it. She watched his every move.

He stood the candle on the base of the upturned tin, and its flaring light threw shadows adance on the curve of the walls. He went to the door and eased out one of the turves. But for a second only. For the storm was raging now with sustained malevolence, and the bank was a place of death, a battleground of wind and spume and ripped-up gravel and sand.

But inside the sod hut it was sheltered and almost cosy. The little boy and the golden seal lay either side of the circle of candlelight and stared at each other.

And the hours passed.

Every now and then Eric pulled aside one of the turves to see if the storm was easing off, but its violence remained unabated, hour after hour. Every now and then he renewed the candles—they burnt fast in the eddying draughts. And in between times he ate chocolate, bar after bar of it. And every time he ate a bar of chocolate he laid out a salmon cut for the golden seal. At first she wouldn't look at it. But eventually, about the time that behind the storm clouds the sun was dipping under the ice-blink, she reached out her neck and sniffed at and tasted the nearest cut. She liked it. The little boy gave her more. And it was not very long before she was letting him put the fish into her mouth.

Come sundown the temperature dropped sharply. The wind backed and the rain hardened to snow. Eric began to shiver. He unearthed the blankets, cached alongside the tin of provisions. There were two of them. He wrapped himself in one and the other he draped carefully over the gold furred seal.

And the hours passed, each slower and colder than the one before.

They lay either side of the hut. Between them the guttering candle, outside the moan of the wind and the drifting up of the snow, and above the storm clouds the anaemic stars creeping conspirator-like into a frightened sky. The night grew darker. The snow drifted higher. The candle burnt lower. Its wick drooped into the melted wax. The flame was snuffed out. A pencil of smoke coiled up to the roof sods. And the little boy slept.

He woke in the small cold hours of the morning, stiff, uncomfortable and trembling. The hut smelt of smoke, candle-grease, fish and excrement, and the gravel was rimmed with frost. He was lost and cold and oh so miserably alone. He tried to wrap himself more warmly into the blanket; but the blanket was all sides and ends—not big enough to keep out the cold. For a while he rocked to and fro, trying to comfort himself. Then he began to cry. He cried noiselessly, the tears welling out in a steady flood, salting his cheeks, trickling round the corners of his mouth and dropping forlornly into a fold in the blanket. It was the loneliness that frightened him most.

On the far side of the hut the golden seal stirred. Her head swayed up; her eyes glowed warm and red.

Eric stopped crying. He stared at the eyes, mesmerized. Then unthinkingly, half-asleep, half-awake, his blanket dragging behind him, he crawled across to her. Awkwardly in the dark he snuggled against her. She was soft and warm and comforting. And she didn't snarl at him.

Soon his shivering, like his tears, died away. And it was not very long before he fell asleep, his face buried deep in the fine-spun gold of her fur.

During the night he slipped lower, and by dawn he was wedged against the warmth of her teats and her pups were snuffling hungrily. She nuzzled him aside. He fell to the ground; the cold and hardness of the stones jerked him awake, and he sat up stretching and yawning.

The air in the sod hut was heavy and stale, and he went to the doorway and tried to ease out the turves. They were stuck. He kicked them impatiently, and they cracked open and ice, wind and snow came swirling into the hut.

It was an unfamiliar world he peered out on. The sky hung low, a livid sheet wiped clear of colouring or cloud, and across it streamed the wind, a wind robbed now of its former malevolence but still strong enough to bowl a man off his feet and to drive in front of it a continuous veil of snow. The storm was dying, but it was not yet dead.

Thoughtfully Eric pulled back the turves; thoughtfully he looked at the seal. And he was troubled. For it came to him that now the weather was improving his father would soon be starting to search for him; and didn't his father often go hunting golden seals—with a gun?

The idea appalled him. It was unthinkable that 'she with the yellow hair' should be hurt. She was his friend. He sat down, head in hands, thinking. And after a while and with delightful clarity the answer came to him. He must make certain he found his father before his father found the golden seal; and he must make him promise never to hurt her.

Having hit on his plan he was eager to be off—at the back of his mind was a nagging fear that his father might appear unexpectedly and shoot the seal before he had a chance to explain. He stuffed the last of the chocolate into his pocket; he fed the last of the fish to the golden seal, and as soon as he could stand against the ever-lessening tear of the wind he set off for the *barabara*.

In the doorway of the hut he paused and looked back. His eyes met the golden seal's.

'Don't you worry,' he said. 'I'll see nobody shoots you.'

6

THE schooner hove-to at the edge of the kelp.
'Eli! Alex!' The voice was clipped and decisive.
'Lower the dory.'

The Aleut deckhands, their faces impassive, paid out the hawsers and the dory dropped smooth and square into the sea.

'Eli! A gun and a coil of rope. Hurry!'

From the masthead Howard Hamilton Crawford, sealer and salmon poacher, took a quick bearing on the golden seal: 025 degrees, range roughly a couple of miles. In the disc of his binoculars he could see her clearly, sunning herself on the kelp, tantalizingly out of range. But he'd get her. He'd get her in the end. In the end he always got what he wanted—or that at least was his reputation, from Darwin to Dutch Harbour and from Panama to Macao. He slid down the mast. A quick tap on the wheelhouse barometer—still falling; a swing over the deck-rail, a slither down the falls and he was cranking the dory's outboard.

'Eli! Alex!'

The Aleuts peered over the rail.

'If the storm blows up, run for it. Don't start lookin' for me. Understand?'

They nodded.

'When it clears, stand in to the tail o' the bank. Wait for me there. O.K?'

Again the impassive nod. Then the outboard was spluttering to life and Crawford was swinging the dory towards the kelp. And the golden seal . . .

An hour later the beat of the outboard slowed, weakened, choked and died; and for the third time Crawford lowered himself over the side and set-to to free the screw. The kelp, sticky and resilient, was hard to dislodge; and by the time he had finished the golden seal had moved farther towards the land; once again she was out of range. He cursed. The kelp was thicker than he had anticipated and the seal warier —probably because she was about to pup. He wiped the salt from his eyes and looked back. And for the first time since leaving the schooner, unease welled up in him, sudden as blood from a knife cut. For the sky to southward had turned strangely hard and bright. Go back, his instinct warned him, while you've still time. But the gold of the seal's fur tempted him on. She's heading for the bank, he told himself. And if she can make it so can I.

But he had reckoned without the kelp.

An hour later the dory was enmeshed in the seaweed morass; Crawford could move neither forward nor back; he was stuck fast as a fly in a spider's web, and straight in the path of the storm.

The dory broached-to about twenty yards off shore and he was flung into the sea.

He struck out for the bank. The undertow sucked him seaward, again and again; but at last he fought clear. Dazed and panting, while great waves pounded his boat to matchwood, he looked about him for shelter. At first he could see none, and the expectation of life drained out of him fast as an ebb tide laying bare the flats of an estuary. Then he saw the chinks of light from the *barabara*. Too far, he thought, I'll never make it. But he knew his only hope was to try. On hands and knees, half-shielding his face against flying gravel,

he began to make for the light. Before he had covered fifty yards, the wind had battered him to the edge of unconsciousness. But he kept on. If only he could get to the light. Howard Hamilton Crawford, he told himself over and over again, you've got to get to that light; if you don't get to that god-damned light you'll die; think of the waste of that. And he crawled on.

Beneath him the gravel shifted uneasily, as loose patches of sand were ripped out from under his body. He was bruised and battered by the flying stones and bowled head over heels by the wind. Most men would have given up: would have lain down thankfully and died. But Crawford wasn't the sort to give up. He kept crawling on.

And at last he came to the *barabara*.

He scrabbled at the door. He levered himself to his feet. He tugged at the latch. Again and again.

A pause. Footsteps. And the door crashed open.

A flood of light, blinding by comparison with the dark of the storm, and two figures thrown into sharp relief: a man with bandaged hands and a girl with frightened eyes. He took a half step forward. Then the gravel smacked into him. Pain knifed through his head. Blackness. And in the blackness the walls of the hut, the bandaged hands and the frightened eyes spinning like catharine wheels in the dark. And he spinning with them: round and down, down and round, into a merciful oblivion.

7

SHE shrank away from him, her hand to her mouth. It was Jim who battened down the door and started to haul him across the floor.

'Give us a hand with him, Tania.'

For a second she stood quite still; then she shivered, the tension ebbed out of her and she picked up the sealer's feet and helped to lift him on to the bed. Jim's hands, bandaged, were clumsy.

'Can you loosen his anorak?'

With the anorak pulled back they could see his face: a young, good-looking face, framed by a mass of dark curly hair and twisted even in unconsciousness in lines of pain.

'Poor devil!' Jim's voice was compassionate. 'A sealer, I reckon. Got himself caught in the kelp.'

Tania nodded. And as she stared at the sealer her apprehension drained slowly away. 'Don't let him in,' she had cried, 'it's the devil;' but he wasn't the least bit devil-like, really. She could see that now. He was a normal human being, an ordinary man. And he was hurt. A trickle of blood was running down from his temple.

She fetched sponge and water. She sat on the edge of the bed. She bathed his face, gently and compassionately. After a while his eyes flickered open. They opened uncertainly at first, then as they met hers they widened. And he stared at her: a long no-more-than-half-focused stare.

She moistened her lips. She moved uneasily.

'Jim! I think he's coming round.'

But by the time Jim Lee had walked across to the bed the sealer's eyes were closed.

The night and the storm were one: dark and violent and never-ending. Sleep was out of the question, for they wanted to search for Eric the moment the wind dropped. So they sat up, hour after hour, killing time, talking, gauging the force of the wind and having a look every now and then at the sealer. On more than one occasion Tania had the suspicion that he was watching them through half-closed eyes; but each time, as soon as she went across to him, the eyes drooped shut, and she told herself she must have been mistaken. Then a little after 2 a.m. he sat up.

He sat up slowly, wincing, holding the side of his head. He peered uncertainly round the *barabara*; then his eyes came to rest on Tania.

'Ah! So it wasn't a dream!'

She jumped to her feet.

'I'll heat you some cocoa.'

'Thanks.' He watched her out of the room then turned abruptly to Jim. 'Your squaw, mister?'

'My wife.'

'Ah!' A pause, then, 'Good of you both to sit up with me.'

'We're sitting up on account of our son. He got himself caught in the storm.'

'That's bad.'

Into the haze and slowly lifting bewilderment of Crawford's return to consciousness there seeped a hint of suspicion. So they were sitting up, were they? They said on account of their son. But mightn't it be, in fact, on account of the golden seal? Mightn't they have seen her land? Mightn't they be waiting for the storm to ease before going out to shoot her? He'd best keep his wits about him.

A rattle of mugs from the kitchen; a pause and Jim walked across to the bed. His voice was curious.

'How come you got caught by the storm, mister?'

Crawford's eyes went wary.

'Damned kelp. Clogged my screw. Couldn't get out of it.'

'Sure. But how come you got *into* it?'

'You're mighty curious, mister.'

Jim laughed.

'Your business. Your life you're playing around with.'

'That's how I figured it.'

Another pause; an awkward silence, and constraint building up between them like flood water rising behind the walls of a dam. Then Tania brought in the cocoa.

But the handing round of the mugs of cocoa didn't dispel the constraint; it merely shifted it, giving it impetus in another direction. For as Tania handed Crawford his cocoa, her eyes were lowered, and she was troubled by feelings she had believed to be long-since dead, left behind eight years ago with the fish-smells, cobbles and waterfront arc-lights of another world.

The sweetness and warmth of the cocoa cleared the sealer's head and brought back his strength. He levered himself off the bed and began to walk up and down, gingerly at first then with growing confidence.

'Seems I'm still in one piece. Guess I was lucky.' He turned to Tania. 'I'll shift off your bed and doss down on the floor.'

'Stay if you like. We're not using the bed tonight.'

He looked at her thoughtfully.

'But of course. You're sittin' up. On account of your daughter.'

'Our son.'

'Sure. I mean son . . . You plan to start searchin' for him soon as the wind drops?'

She nodded.

'I think,' Crawford said softly, 'that I'll come with you.'

Jim looked at him curiously.

'Thanks, mister. But you've no occasion to.'

'But I'd like to.' Crawford's voice was bland. 'This search of yours is somethin' I sure wouldn't want to miss.'

He made a great business of making himself comfortable and settling down for the night. But he didn't sleep. And Jim and Tania knew it. At first they were merely suspicious; but after a time they were certain. The stillness was self-willed, the heavy breathing was simulated, the half-closed eyes were watching them, hour after hour.

They tried to slip out without him—the search for Eric was something they would have preferred to do alone. But he heard their snow-shoes swishing across the floor and swung himself off the bed.

'Hey! Wait for me.'

'Wind's still pretty nasty. You sure you want to come?'

'Oh yes. I want to come real bad.'

Soon the two men and the girl, leaning against the wind, were plodding into knee-deep snow. As they struck into the open Jim turned for a moment to look back at the *barabara*; and as he turned he noticed, out of the corner of his eye, Crawford transferring something from one oilskin pocket to another. The early morning light glinted coldly on the barrel of what, to Jim Lee, looked like a ·45 Webley.

8

THE wind was still strong enough to rip off an occasional flurry of snow, but it was possible to stand in it and to walk, and visibility was good. Moving slowly over the soft uneven drifts, the three plodded down to the river. It was impassable. The ankle-deep trickle of yesterday had swollen overnight to an angry torrent, a full thirty yards across. They paused, uncertain what to do next.

'Up-stream.' Jim's shout was submerged in the roar of wind and water; but they followed his lead and struck inland, anxiously scanning the farther bank in the direction of the sod huts. And almost at once Crawford began to lag behind—loath to leave the shore. Jim and Tania couldn't be bothered with him; he had come uninvited; he dropped back unregretted. They had thoughts only for Eric.

Half a mile inland—a little beyond the salmon traps—the river widened, zigzagging from side to side in a miniature flood plain. In several places it was a good sixty yards across, and so silted up with sand-bars that it was usually possible to cross dryshod by jumping from bar to bar. But the bars were submerged now, and between them the water ran fast and deep. They came to a halt, panting, shading their eyes against the sting of the wind. And as they paused, wondering how to cross, Jim reached for Tania's hand.

'Look!' He pointed to the far side of the river; his voice was hushed as a communicant's.

Away on the skyline a pinpoint figure was crossing the dunes.

'Eric!' Tania covered her face. 'Oh, thank God.' And

the tears she had been holding back so long came flooding out unchecked and unashamed.

They were standing on the bank waving at the figure—now running excitedly towards them—when Crawford came plodding up-river.

'Your boy?'

Jim nodded.

So—the sealer was surprised—they really had come to look for their son; and he'd have sworn they were after the golden seal. Not that it mattered; in fact it made things easier; once the family were reunited he'd slip off and start a search of his own. He turned to Jim.

'How you figure to get across to him?'

'Going to be quite a job.' Jim dipped an arm into the river, gauging its coldness and the strength of its flow. 'Here's the likeliest place to ford. Unless we head five or six miles upstream.'

While they were talking, the little boy came running down to the farther bank. He danced about, excitedly, shouting; but what he was saying was lost in the roar of the river.

The idea of trekking half a dozen miles up-stream didn't appeal to Crawford; he was eager to be after the golden seal. He eyed the rope which Jim Lee was uncoiling from round his waist.

'How much you got there?'

'Two-fifty feet.'

'Maybe I could swim across with it.'

'My boy. My swim.'

'With those hands!'

Jim nodded. 'Thanks, mister. But I'll manage.' He laid down the rope and began to strip off the bandages.

Tania's eyes widened. 'Jim! Your hands! You won't get a grip on the rope.' She licked her lips. 'Let me go. Please.' Over her husband's shoulder her eyes met Crawford's: a half-pleading, half-challenging, 'You're-a-man-aren't-you-why-don't-you-do-something' look.

Jim went on unrolling the bandages. 'Quit fussing, Tania. I'll be all right.'

Her concern touched him; but even as he looked at her he saw her anxiety replaced by a slow, satisfied smile. He spun round. But too late. Crawford, the rope hitched round his waist, was already knee-deep in the water. He tossed the loose end to Tania.

MW.

'Belay to the rhododendrons.'

She clove-hitched the rope, quickly and efficiently. And short of trying to haul him back by force there was nothing Jim Lee could do. Angrily he paced the bank.

'Let's hope he knows what he's doing!'

He glanced at Tania. She was watching the sealer. Her lips were parted and her eyes were unusually bright.

47

Crawford made steady progress. He knew what he was doing all right—Jim had to admit that. He struck off at an angle up-stream, he picked a good route and he chose the right places to ford the channels. Most of the time he was no more than waist to shoulder deep, leaning up-river against the force of the flood; but every now and then he had to swim. Those were the moments of danger: when his head disappeared, the rope jerked taut and he was swept down-stream in the creaming ice-cold flood. But he was a powerful swimmer. He fought his way methodically from bar to bar. Soon he was two-thirds of the way across.

Jim relaxed. 'He's going to make it.' He glanced again at Tania. A quick glance only. Then he looked away, prey to a sudden complexity of doubts and jealousies and fears. On whose account was she breathing so fast? Eric's or Crawford's? For whom were the starry eyes and the tight-clenched hands?

On the farther bank Crawford crawled out of the water. He shook himself like a dog and looked about for the boy—a moment before he'd been down at the water's edge, dancing and shouting encouragement; but now, realizing the swimmer wasn't his father, he had drawn back. Crawford went up to him.

'Hullo, young man. I've come to give you a hand across.'

Eric shifted uneasily. 'Why didn't my Dad come?'

'Your Dad hurt his hands in the storm. Not real bad. Just bad enough to stop him hangin' on to a rope.'

The boy accepted this. He looked the sealer up and down, noting the bandage round his head.

'You get hurt in the storm too? Like my Dad?'

'Sure did. You like to see?'

He took off the bandages and showed the little boy his bruise. Eric became suddenly confidential.

'Guess what happened to *me* in the storm!'

'You get a bruise too?'

'Not a bruise. Something much, much, *much* better. Something I found. I'll give you three guesses.'

'You find a bag o' gold?'

The boy jumped up and down with delight. 'You're warm, mister. You're real warm.'

'A bag o' diamonds, then?'

'No'—scornfully—'you're cold now.'

An idea, an utterly fantastic idea, flashed through Crawford's mind. Could he have found the golden seal? But no. Of course he couldn't. If he had, he wouldn't still be alive. Faintly above the roar of the river he heard a shout from the farther bank. He looked up and saw the scar-faced man and his squaw waving anxiously.

'Your Mum an' Dad's getting impatient.' He started to haul in the slack of the rope. 'We'd better be headin' back. Now you know how to ride pick-a-back?'

'Sure I know. But what about your third guess? For what I found?'

'I'll save that one up.' Crawford's voice was thoughtful. 'I'm going to think about that one real hard while we're crossin' the river.'

With the slack of the rope he strapped Eric across his back: wrists to shoulders, ankles to the back of his thighs. Then he waded into the water.

The second crossing was more difficult than the first, much more difficult. Eric was heavy. His weight threw Crawford off balance, and his bulk made greater resistance to the force of the flood. Three times the sealer lost his footing; three times he was carried down-stream; and three times only the tautening rope saved him from being swept out to the estuary. Half-way across he began to wonder if he was going to make it; for he was gasping for breath and a numbing cramp was clutching his legs. But he willed himself on, clawing at the rope hand over hand, until quite suddenly the bank was very near and the scar-faced man was in the water beside him, breaking the force of the flood, guiding him through the tangle of rhododendrons and finally hauling him on to ground which was wonderfully stable and firm.

He lay face down in the snow, panting, shivering, no more than half-conscious of what was happening around him: the anxious questions of the parents, the excited chatter of the little boy. He was paid out, exhausted, oppressed by a feeling of anti-climax; he'd been a fool to risk his life—just for the sake of the challenge in a pretty girl's eyes. And see how grateful she was! Fussing over her son, leaving him flat on his face in the snow.

An arm slid unexpectedly under his shoulders. Fingers, cool and gentle, rearranged the bandages round his head, and a trickle of brandy ran like liquid fire down his throat. He looked up.

Her lips were less than a hand's-breadth from his; her eyes were soft and gentle and she was giving him the same strange disconcerting look that she had given him several times before in the *barabara*. It was a look which he, being a man of the world, knew how to interpret; he had been the recipient of it before: when at season's end the salmon fleet came back from the traps and the chi-chi girls were waiting clustered as moths beneath the Dutch Harbour arc-lights, their eyes (like the squaw-girl's) part challenge, part curiosity and part defiance.

He looked at her with a new awareness.

'Thank you'—her voice was soft—'for bringing him back.'

His hand clamped down on her wrist. He let his fingers dig into her flesh. He let his eyes run over her, stripping her.

'A pleasure.' His fingers tightened. 'A real pleasure.'

He was surprised when her eyes turned suddenly frightened. She jerked away from him, upsetting the bottle of brandy. She scrambled to her feet. Her voice was breathless.

'Jim! Let's be headin' back.'

Of course! Her husband! He was a fool to have forgotten she had a husband only a few dozen yards away. Apprehension welled up in him. But a glance at the man with the scar and he was reassured. For Jim Lee, apparently oblivious to all else, was deep in talk with his son.

9

A S they walked back to the *barabara* the little boy tugged at his father's arm.

'What's up, Eric?'

'I got a secret, Dad.' His eyes slid round to the others. 'A secret for you.'

They dropped back—there couldn't be any harm, Jim thought, in dropping back; so long as they kept the others in sight. As soon as they were out of earshot, Eric began to hop up and down.

'Promise me something, Dad.'

Jim looked at his son. He had been wondering how to work round to the subject of promises.

'Talking of promising things, Eric, I guess you got some explaining to do.'

'Yes, Dad.' Then, half-heartedly, 'But I didn't really go out of sight of the house. I could see it all the time. In the glasses.'

At that, Jim Lee read his son a little lecture—he knew it sounded pompous, but that was something which couldn't be helped—all about the importance of honouring the spirit of a promise as well as the letter. And Eric said he understood and was sorry. And that was that.

Then—cheerfully—'An' now will *you* make a promise, Dad?'

'What do you want me to promise?'

A long pause: then—breathlessly—'I found something, Dad. Something extra special. If I tell you what I found, will you promise never, never, *never* to hurt her?

'All right then.'

'Cross your heart?'

'Yes. Sure I'll cross my heart.' He was preoccupied and impatient to catch up with the others. What Eric had found couldn't, he told himself, be all that important; certainly not as important as that look he had seen the sealer giving his wife. His attention was more than half on Tania and Crawford, now a full fifty yards ahead, when—suddenly—he realized what Eric was saying.

'. . . an' her fur's all soft and yellow like the sun. An' she's got two sweet little babies. An' she's a *golden seal*, Dad. An' she's my friend. An' I'm going to have her for all my very own, like boys in other countries have a dog.'

He stood suddenly very still. 'What? Say that again.'

'I found a gold seal, Dad. A real live Mummy golden seal. An' she's my friend.'

He sat down. For eight years this was what he had worked and planned and dreamed for. For eight years he had scoured the bank in sun and snow and blizzard and mist. For eight years his dream had been unfulfilled. Now at last he had the chance to fulfil it; to buy the transmitting set, the outboard motor, the stove; to toss the two-thousand dollar pelt on to the bar of the Cornucopia. The cost? The breaking of a carelessly given promise. He looked at his son.

'But Eric! A golden seal's a wild animal. Like a bear. You can't have one for a pet.'

'I can't?'

'No, you *certainly* can't. I'm sorry, son. But that's the way it is.'

A long silence, then bravely—'Anyway, guess I don't care so much 'bout her not being a pet. Not now I know for sure that nobody's going to hurt her.'

And he took his father's hand.

10

HOT meal, a change of clothes and Crawford was eager to be off. He stood at the *barabara* window watching the signs of the dying storm: the paling sky, the lessening wind, the puffs of cloud (harbingers of the cold front swinging round in the hurricane's wake) scudding low over the tail of the bank like smoke rings from a battery of discharging cannon.

'Weather's clearin'.' His voice was casual.

Jim nodded.

'Think I'll take a stroll outside. Jest to have a look round.'

At that a suspicion which had been building up for some time in Jim Lee's mind was confirmed. So the sealer *was* after something; odds were it was 'she with the yellow hair'.

They didn't try to dissuade him. They watched the tall oilskinned figure striding purposefully down to the shore. Tania was puzzled.

'What does he hope to find?'

Jim pulled open a drawer and took out a revolver: a Colt ·38.

'Listen, Tania! I want you to carry this. As long as he's on the island.'

'Oh Jim! I can look after myself without a gun!'

'There's no harm in being prepared.'

She looked from the gun to her husband and back again. Then with a little grimace she dropped the Colt into the pocket of her skirt.

'Happier?'

Her voice was half grateful, half amused.

'Yes, much happier. And I'll tell you why. Eric and me are leaving you a while. We're going back to the sod hut where he spent the night.'

She reached for his hand.

'Jim! What *is* going on?'

He looked at her, undecided. Should he tell her about the golden seal, about his promise to Eric and his suspicion of Crawford? But it was all so indefinite as yet.

'I'm not sure right now,' he said slowly, 'what's going on myself. But when I *am*, I promise I'll tell you. O.K?'

She was none too happy about it; he could see that. But she nodded and went off, at his request, to make up a pack of chocolate and salmon cuts for reprovisioning the sod hut.

A few minutes later father and son were heading inland. They forded the river high up and cut back to the sod hut via the lower slopes of Shishaldin. The moment the circle of turves came in sight, the little boy began to hop up and down like a wallaby.

'Come on, Dad! Run!'

But Jim Lee halted. He unslung his rifle.

'Now listen, Eric. This golden seal may be a friend of yours. But she doesn't know me. So we've got to be careful, see.'

They approached the hut with all the care and circumspection of a patrol reconnoitring an enemy strongpoint. Then came the anti-climax. The golden seal wasn't there.

Had Crawford beaten them to it? That was Jim's first conclusion. Yet he had been listening carefully and had heard no shot, and hadn't the sealer when last seen been heading in the opposite direction? Was the whole thing, then, a little boy's dream? But no: the excrement and the strands of golden fur precluded that. So there was only one answer; the seal must, in the last couple of hours, have left the sod hut of her own free will.

They cleaned the hut and restocked it with food, then they set about to trail her.

The lagoons, Jim decided, were the most likely place: the shallow ribbons of water necklaced between the bank and the foothills of Shishaldin.

The lagoons were not large but they were reed-fringed and hard to search. Armed with six-foot stems of bullrush, father and son poked and prodded along either bank. At first they were confident of finding her. But at the end of an hour they were nearing the point where the lagoons degenerated into a wilderness of marsh and quicksand. And there was still no sign of the golden seal.

Eric flopped down, exhausted and near to tears.

'She's not here, Dad. Guess she's gone back to the sea.'

Jim looked at the forty-foot rollers still pounding the length of the beach. His voice was puzzled. 'She wouldn't take new-born pups into a sea like that.'

For a while there was silence. Eric's bullrush, disconsolate, swished the water; drips patterned the lagoon in widening circles; their shape—perfectly symmetrical—reminded him of something; he had a feeling it was something important. And suddenly he got it.

'I know!' He jumped to his feet. 'Secret Water!'

He had only seen the pool once, but he had never forgotten it. The perfect circle of green set emerald-like in the shaft of an extinct volcano—one of Shishaldin's offshoots, thrust up unexpectedly in the middle of the sandhills. It was the ideal hideout. For who would expect to find water on top of a sandhill!

Jim had doubts; but his son's enthusiasm was infectious and before long they were wading through the lagoons and striking up the 200-foot ridge of sand. As they neared the crest the little boy broke away and ran eagerly ahead.

'Careful, Eric.'

At the top of the rise the boy froze, too intent even to

motion his father to silence. In an instant Jim was beside him.

And she was there.

She had heard them coming and wedged herself under a ledge of rock, her pups behind her.

The little boy slithered down to the water. 'Don't be frightened. It's only me.'

Jim Lee cocked his rifle. His voice was sharp. 'Eric! Don't go near her.'

'It's all right, Dad. She knows *me*.'

Out of his pocket he pulled a cut of salmon, saved from the cache in the sod hut. He tossed it into the pool.

For a full minute the golden seal didn't move. Then in a sudden swirl the salmon was gone.

Eric jumped up and down in delight. 'Come on! I've got lots more here!' He held out another cut—just as he had done in the sod hut. And the golden seal swam to the edge of the pool, reached up and took the fish, very gently, out of his hand.

On the trigger of his rifle Jim's finger tightened. His sights were between the golden seal's eyes. Wasn't this the moment he'd been hoping for, the moment of danger, the moment when he could kill the seal and then say afterwards, 'I only did it, Eric, to stop her attacking you.' His finger curled. He felt the give of the first pressure. But at the final tightening squeeze, he baulked. Inside his brain a voice was hammering, 'Shoot her, you fool, shoot her; two thousand dollars, a transmitting set in case your wife is ill, an outboard motor to save your life on a lee shore, a stove to stop you freezing in winter, drinks for the house in the Cornucopia and admiration in the eyes of the men who have shunned you.' But his finger refused the final squeeze. His sights wavered. Suddenly he couldn't see the gold furred seal any more; he could see only his son's face, uplifted trustingly to his. And he knew at that moment that as he had promised so it would

be: never, never, never would he hurt the golden seal. He laid his rifle aside.

The Kodiak bear that sat patiently watching the pool was old, purblind and stumpy-toothed, and a bullet wound in his groin made him move stiffly with a drunken crab-like lurch. But his claws were long and still sharp as Toledo steel; and he was as cunning as the proverbial serpent.

The storm had played havoc with his usual hunting ground, driving the snowshoe rabbits into their burrows and the foxes down to the lowered snowline; and before long the bear was hungry. His instinct led him then down to the shore, down to the mouth of the estuary where the salmon would soon be spawning and he'd be able to sit on the river bank scooping a banquet out of the seething morass of fish. But the salmon this autumn were late in spawning—delayed by the drought—and it wasn't long before the bear, of necessity, was thinking of food of a different kind. He had seen the man and the boy traversing the dunes. He had seen them disappear into the waterhole. Patiently he lurched his way downwind. Patiently in the shadow of a sharply rising sand-dune he squatted on his haunches, waiting.

As they pulled out from the waterhole Jim looked back at the gold furred seal.

'I guess,'—his voice was casual—'I guess we'd best keep her hideout a secret.'

'A secret? Just 'tween you and me?'

'Just between you and me and Mummy.'

Eric was surprised. 'You mean not tell Uncle Howard?'

'No,'—with careful emphasis—'I wouldn't tell Uncle Howard. In fact Uncle Howard would be the very last person I'd tell.'

As they headed back for the *barabara* Jim was preoccupied. He found himself listening: listening for the sound of a shot, for the sharp stiletto crack of Tania's revolver. His attention was on other things than picking a route. Nevertheless, he sheered away from the patch of shadow at the foot of the steep-sided sandhill. He sheered away from it not by design but by instinct, by the hunter's innate avoidance of dead ground. And as he altered course, the sun came palely out through a rift in the cloud; and the bear, caught in the unwelcome light, drew in his head.

Jim Lee, jerked out of his meditation, stared at the patch of shadow; and saw, aglint in the sun, the polished curve of the Kodiak's claws.

He knew enough about bears to be frightened.

He weighed the odds—the fact that Kodiaks were often shortsighted; the fact that he and Eric were to windward; the fact that his rifle—a ·330—was too light to be reliable; the difficult ground; the noise of the sea. Then he grabbed Eric. He didn't speak. He raised a finger to his lips and pointed to the shore, and they backed, slowly and soundlessly, away from the sandhill.

The bear couldn't see them. But he knew they were escaping. He padded after them, his muzzle lifting this way and that like a radar scanner questing its target. But Jim and Eric had the weather gauge of him. They worked their way down to the shore, to where the pound of the surf muffled the crunch of their footsteps and the off-shore wind swirled their scent out to sea. Here, on the edge of the breakers, they waited.

A little to their right a skein of sea-fowl rose soundlessly and were wheeled away in the wind. A moment later the Kodiak topped the bank. He was angry and thwarted: baulked for the moment of his expected meal. He padded up and down. His purblind eyes stared at them sightlessly. His nostrils flared angrily as he searched for their scent. Twice he came lurching down to the water's edge—once within thirty yards of them. But he could neither hear them, scent them nor see them. And at last he gave up. With an angry disappointed cough he lurched away in the direction of the *barabara*.

But Jim was taking no chances. For a full ten minutes he and Eric stood motionless; and when at last they moved off they trod slowly and cautiously, synchronizing their footsteps with the backwash of the waves. And all the way back to the estuary they stayed close to the sea, they avoided dead ground, and Jim kept his rifle cocked and at the ready. He had a very healthy respect for Kodiaks.

He was in fact so preoccupied with avoiding the bear that all other thoughts—the golden seal and his promise, the sealer and his wife—were driven temporarily out of his head.

The crack of the revolver came as a surprise: a surprise too shocking, for a moment, to be believed in, like the sudden resurgence of a ghost that one believes to be laid.

For a second he stood stockstill, rooted in disbelief. Then

he began to run. He ran fast: so fast that Eric couldn't keep pace with him.

'Dad! Dad! Wait for me!' The little boy was frightened.

But Jim Lee ran on. More urgent and more compelling than the fear in his son's voice was the fear in his heart: the fear that fountained up, like blood from a severed artery, too frightening to be believed.

II

AS Crawford headed down to the shore his hopes were high. The gold furred seal was on the island; the others knew nothing about her; she was as good as his.

At the mouth of the estuary he paused. Two ways were open to him. To westward was the tail of the bank—a couple of miles of shingle and sand ending (at the island's south-west corner) in a projecting underwater spit; and to eastward, across the river, was the main reach of the bank—some eighteen miles of sand-dune backed by the lagoons and the lower slopes of Shishaldin. When Crawford had last seen the golden seal she was heading straight for the mouth of the estuary. It was a toss up which side she had landed.

He turned west—he'd try the easy side first. Climbing a sand-dune he scanned the tail of the bank. He scanned it methodically, section by section, searching for the tell-tale glitter of gold. But the bank was all aglitter with gold: a kaleidoscope of yellows and browns, patterned by cloud shadows and ever shifting to the take-off and landing of birds. She'll be hard to spot, he thought; until I get near: then I'll see her all right. He began to work his way along the shore in a series of careful zigzags between dunes and sea.

At first he walked fast, hopefully, his footsteps crunching crisply across the gravel. But loose-packed stones are tiring to plod through, disappointment is a sure sapper of energy, and as he worked his way farther and farther west and there was still no sign of the golden seal, his steps became increasingly weary, until at the end of a couple of hours he slumped exhausted and disconsolate on to the neck of the sandpit. His search had been unrewarded.

So, he thought, I guessed wrong, she must be the other side of the estuary. He cursed. The search was not going to be as easy as he had hoped.

An hour later, rested but in none too good a temper, he was plodding back.

As he retraced his steps he put the golden seal out of his mind (she wasn't on this part of the bank so there was no object in worrying over her) and his thoughts turned to the family he had stumbled across so unexpectedly. Theirs, he reflected, must be a queer sort of life; all right perhaps for the man—he probably did pretty well with a virgin island to trap—but damnably dull for the squaw-girl. He wondered how she stuck it, an attractive little thing cooped up year after year with a scar-faced fellow old enough to be her father. How she must long for a break, for excitement, change—wasn't the interest she'd shown in him proof of that? And as his thoughts coalesced round the girl to the exclusion of everything else, so insidiously ideas which had been lying fallow in his mind came pushing through to the surface, like snakes rearing their heads from a clutch of eggs that is warmed by the heat of the sun. And he reminded himself, with pleasure, of the way that physical awareness had been growing up between himself and the girl, step by step: her frightened eyes staring at him through the tumult of the storm; her hands cool and gentle bathing his face; and on the bank of the river her parted lips less than a hand's-breadth from his. He reminded himself too of the looks she had given him; the speculative half-challenging looks; the looks that he, being a man of the world, knew how to interpret. And the snakes twisted this way and that and warmed themselves in the sun of his imagination.

It wasn't long before he found himself back at the mouth of the estuary.

He looked at the sky and judged that it needed less than two hours to the fall of the brief sub-arctic twilight. He looked at the sea and judged it still too high for the Aleuts to be heading back with his schooner (and even when they did head back it would probably take them several days to beat up to the island against wind and head sea). He looked at the bank on the farther side of the river, and the ground appeared loose and uninviting, and the golden seal, he told himself, would still be there tomorrow. He looked up-stream at the *barabara* and there in the porch he spotted the squaw-girl, at work on some sort of wickerwork basket. And she was alone.

For a moment he stood irresolute. Then a memory that had been stirring for some time at the back of his mind came welling to the surface, and he remembered the sealers' gossip in the Cornucopia (he had hardly bothered to listen to it at the time) about the man who had married a chi-chi girl from a harbour brothel and gone off with her to live on an uninhabited island. Of course. This was the man. And the girl.

So! She not only looked like a chi-chi girl, she *was* one. That, of course, made everything pleasurably simple.

As he walked up-river a familiar dryness tightened the back of his throat.

She looked up. He was no more than a couple of paces away, watching her from behind the rail of the porch.

'Hullo!' Her voice was startled. 'Enjoy your walk?'

'So so.' His eyes shifted from her face to the wickerwork basket. 'What you doin' there?'

'Mending a salmon trap. Got bust in the storm.'

He sat himself down beside her. 'I'll give you a hand.' He picked up a slither of willow and pushed it in through the latticework opening.

She looked at him. Her voice was mocking. 'Sure you know how?'

'I know how. As well as you do.' He smiled at her, an admiring confident smile.

And she lowered her eyes.

'All right,' she said. 'I'll let you.'

And she took the end of the willow and started to work it in and out through the transverse bars of the trap, like a spinner weaving a weft. She worked dexterously and fast. But no matter how fast she worked he kept pace with her, feeding the slithers of willow into the basket in a smooth rhythmic sequence. After a while she glanced at him: downwards and sideways.

'You've done this sort of thing before!'

'And why not!'

Again the lowered eyes.

This, he told himself, was going to be easy.

Then unexpectedly she shivered, and as he fed in the next length of willow she didn't take it but stopped it with the palm of her hand. She stood up.

'My husband'll be back soon.' Her voice was matter of fact. 'I'd better be getting some food.'

His hand closed over her wrist. 'Forget your husband, Tania.'

'I don't want to. Her voice had gone suddenly breathless.

'You sure you don't?'

'No. I mean yes. I *am* sure.'

He was pleased to see that the mocking eyes had turned suddenly frightened. She backed away from him. She blundered into the rail of the porch. And as she half lost her balance he grabbed her. He pulled her towards him, until her lips once again were less than a hand's-breadth from his; and this time there was no Peeping Tom of a husband to spoil his fun. He let his fingers dig into the flesh of her arms. He felt her go limp. It was what he'd expected—she was a squaw, wasn't she, *and* a chi-chi girl? His mouth reached for hers. For a second he felt himself poised—like a surf-rider

65

under whose board the comber is trembling—poised on the threshold of a familiar triumph.

And at that second she spat in his face.

The monstrous unexpectedness of it broke his grip, and she squirmed away from him. He reached for her again in blind fury. For a moment he was too beside himself to realize what she was saying. Then the words got through.

'Keep back. Or I'll kill you.'

And he pulled up short. For the revolver was trained on his stomach.

His hands opened and closed. His voice was thick. 'Quit actin' the frightened virgin.'

Her voice was low, almost a whisper: 'Those whom God has joined together let no man put asunder.'

He stared at her. 'Jesus Christ! A Bible pushin' squaw.'

Her eyes were angry. 'I didn't think you'd understand.'

'I understand one thing all right—all those come-hither looks you been givin' me! I understand them fine now. You're a frigid cheatin' tease.'

Childlike she stamped her foot. 'I'm not. I can't help the way I look. But don't you see, it's wrong.'

An old Aboriginal saying flashed through Crawford's mind: 'If man wants woman . . . can't help . . . must have.' And he knew at that moment that certain as sun-up follows night there were two things he was going to have before he left Unimak: the golden seal and the squaw-girl.

He looked at her, a shrewd calculating look. In spite of her gun, in spite of her Bible quoting, she wanted him. That he was sure of. He took a half-pace towards her. He raised his hands over his head.

'Look at me, Tania.' His voice was soft. 'You wouldn't shoot a man with his hands raised, would you?'

She backed away. 'I'll kill you.' Her eyes flickered this way and that like frightened mice. 'Take one more step and I'll kill you.'

Bluff! His vanity wouldn't have it be anything else. All this talking! There'd be no time for talking when he got his hands on her. He took a step forward. And another.

He was so close to her that the crack of the revolver almost split his eardrums; an acrid spiral of smoke swirled past his face, and the impact of the bullet jerked him round like a top. He felt no pain. Only a sense of incredulous outrage: that he, Howard Hamilton Crawford, should have been rejected and shot by a squaw. He waited for the pain; but it didn't come. He looked down and saw the charred groove where bullet and gunflash had ploughed through shirt and anorak less than an inch from his hip. Somehow, from a range of less than three feet, she had managed to miss him.

Relief flooded over him. Then anger: a cold, hard, calculating anger. He looked at her with sudden hatred.

'You little bitch. I'll make you pay for that.'

He pushed past her, into the *barabara*. He slid into a chair, breathing heavily. After a while he took off his anorak and began to run his fingers along the charred groove: up and down, up and down, disbelievingly. He was vaguely aware that the girl, from the doorway, was watching him.

'You all right?'

He nodded.

'We'll have to explain the shot.'

'Explain it?' In a disinterested sort of way he was surprised.

'Yes, explain it. My husband—' A pause: then, breathlessly, 'If he knew it was you I'd fired at, he'd kill you.'

He looked at her and a slow and mirthless smile spread over his face. 'Oh no, Tania.' His soft voice was soft, almost gentle. 'Oh no, Tania. You've got it the wrong way round. I'd kill him.'

Her face whitened and her tongue ran over her lips. Her fear brought him a thrill of pleasure, a mite of recompense; hadn't he promised to make her pay?

'I'm younger than he is, Tania. And stronger.' He watched her wilt under the soft insinuating words as if from a flurry of blows. 'And I've got a sort of reputation with knives and guns.'

She stared at him, twisting and untwisting her hands; then the words came tumbling out in a frightened flood. 'I'll tell him the gun went off by accident. No, I know. I'll tell him I fired at a bear: a Kodiak bear.'

'He'll not believe you, Tania.'

'Yes,'—with unexpected certainty—'he'll believe me. I know.'

He realized that the thought of her husband's trust in her had given her new confidence. He couldn't, for the moment, hurt her more.

'Spin him any story you like. It's no concern of mine.' He turned his back on her and began to take off his boots.

For a moment she stared at him, undecided; then she snatched up his anorak; she stuffed it into a cupboard, grabbed a rifle and rushed out of the hut. From the doorway he watched her, her hair streaming out behind her, running down to the mouth of the estuary.

The river had fallen six feet in as many hours, and Jim was fording it, Eric riding pick-a-back. She helped them ashore.

She found her husband easier to convince about the bear than she had dared to hope. At first she couldn't think why he was accepting her story so readily and so without reservation. Then the little boy's chatter got suddenly through to her.

'An' wasn't he fierce and horrible and simply 'normous, Mummy! And do you know, *he was after us too*!'

At that she sat down on the bank, not knowing whether to laugh or cry. And when Jim took her in his arms she clung to him very closely, as though she could never bring herself to let him go.

12

WHEN Crawford, Jim and Tania sat down to supper the tinder for a conflagration was ready and waiting. But the spark to ignite it was never struck. And the reason was tiredness.

The tempo of events had caught up with them all. Storm and the fear of bereavement, lack of sleep and the nearness of death, covetousness, temptation and lust: of these in the last twenty-four hours they had had their fill. Now as darkness closed in on the island few if any of their problems were solved. But they were too tired to care. The moment the meal was finished, as though in obedience to an implicit truce, they started to doss down for the night. And sleep, in a welcome flood of oblivion, came to them soon.

But sleep brings dreams. All those in the *barabara* dreamed that night. The dreams of the adults were troubled. They tossed and turned and plucked at their bedclothes, prey to a complexity of hopes and fears. Only the dreams of the little boy were innocent, as he played with the gold furred seal in waters seething with salmon and lovely as those which ran out, long ago, from Eden.

Jim Lee woke in the still of the false dawn. He woke suddenly, all-of-a-piece, listening. At the far end of the *barabara* a door closed softly; a pause, then footsteps crunching in *diminuendo* across the gravel. He slipped out of bed; he tiptoed across to a window.

Crawford, carrying a gun, was heading towards the lagoons.

Jim watched him out of sight, then thoughtfully he walked back to the bed. He looked at Tania. She was still asleep. Her face was pale, withdrawn and unhappy. He bent down and kissed her lips. In her sleep she moved uneasily. 'No,' she whispered. 'Please.' She rolled over and buried her face in the pillow. And as he looked at her, wondering, all the doubts and fears of yesterday came slithering back, like many-legged insects crawling out of the slime of a nightmare pond. Slowly and without waking her, he dressed. Slowly, as the sun swung huge and gold out of the sea, he left the *barabara* and climbed a little way up the bank.

Never had Unimak looked more beautiful. Sunrise and high tide, a cooling wind straight off the sea, combers of rainbow hue pounding the shore and the pinions of the wheeling sea-fowl tipped with vermilion and gold. Of the storm the only traces left were the waves and the sea kelp; and these too would soon be no more than a memory—the waves smoothed to a crinkle, the sea kelp buried beneath the sand. But what of the flotsam cast up by the storm? The golden seal and the sealer? They threatened to remain: unwanted, alien and disruptive, the serpents in Arcady, the destroyers of all that he held most dear.

He picked up a handful of stones and let them run through his fingers. So, he thought, are the sands of my happiness threatening to run dry as the man whose life we saved in the storm makes calf's eyes at my wife and she smiles back at him and I, poor cuckold fool, do nothing. And the devil whispered in his ear, 'Take your gun. Shoot the seal. And then the man will leave, and things will be as they were before.'

And he was tempted.

And the voice of the devil whispered on; eloquent, persuasive, eminently reasonable: 'You'd not be doing it for the 2,000 dollars. You'd be doing it to get rid of the sealer, to protect your wife. One shot, one single shot between the eyes and everything will be solved.'

And the temptation scoured through his mind like a tide rip.

And yet still, obstinately and against all the dictates of common sense, he baulked at breaking his promise. Still— blindly, unreasoningly and contrary to all expediency—he clung to the one fact in a sea of doubt that he was sure of: it was sinful to break a promise, especially a promise to a child. And sin was wicked. Sin couldn't be right. Sin was what drove Adam and Eve out of Eden. And as his certainty gained strength, so the whispering of the devil died slowly away in the pound of combers along the shore and he knew quite suddenly that nothing—no, not even the threatened spoliation of all that he held most dear—could persuade him ever to break the promise he had given to his son.

Having made his decision he felt a sudden lightening of spirit, like a man who has passed through a street of harlots and kept his innocence. He sat down, chin in hands, thinking. There must surely be some other way of solving the problem. And as idea after idea came, was rejected and then forgotten, it gradually dawned on him that the problem was one he shouldn't have been tackling alone; it was Tania's as much— if not more than—his. It occurred to him too that a deal of heartache might have been avoided if he had talked things over with her before. But better, he told himself as he walked thoughtfully back to the *barabara*, better late than never.

As he neared the house he saw that she was not, as he had expected, still in bed but was dressed and sitting in the porch among a litter of salmon traps. And he saw, too, that she had been crying.

When, half-asleep and half-awake, she reached for him and found him gone she was terrified. She slid out of bed. Cold with fear she ran to the kitchen. She eased open the door. And her fears were confirmed. Crawford had vanished too.

A nightmare scene built up in her mind: the two men in the half-light of dawn tramping the bank, the provocative taunt, the angry reply, the knife stab in the back, the gold of the gravel incarnadined with her husband's blood and she so very far away. Trembling, she ran from window to window, searching for a clue as to which way they had gone. And at the last window she saw him, less than a hundred yards from the *barabara*, sitting chin in hands on the crest of a sand-dune.

She dressed slowly, automatically, drained of all emotion except an unthinking relief. She took a chair into the porch (she could see her husband from there) and sat down beside the half-mended salmon traps. After a while, to give herself something to do, she began to feed the lengths of willow in and out through the trap bars: in and out, in and out. And as she worked memories of yesterday came crowding back. And before long, mixed up with the memories, was the voice of the devil whispering in her ear. 'In spite of what happened yesterday you want him. You know you want him. And what's the harm in it? Your husband need never know.' And she screwed up her eyes and the willow strips slid in and out, faster and faster. And the voice of the devil whispered on, quiet, persistent and traitorously reasonable. 'Eight years with hardly a glimpse of another man. No wonder you feel the way you do!' And the willow strips slid in and out. And the voice went whispering on. 'And you can't help your feelings, can you? Once a chi-chi girl, always a chi-chi girl.' And tears pricked at the back of her eyes. And the voice of the devil was triumphant. 'In any case, it's too late to draw back now. In your heart you've committed adultery already. Whether or not you give him your body as well is unimportant.' And at that, the words she had been trying desperately to recall came flooding back, and once again she was in Dutch Harbour in the green-domed, red-roofed Church of Saint Peter repeating the words of the Priest, 'And forsaking all others keep thee only unto me.' She repeated the promise now, over and over again: 'Keep thee only unto me, keep thee only unto me.' At first the words were all but meaningless, like a parrot-learned poem; but in time they brought her comfort. And then strength. She flung down the salmon trap. The voice of the devil was stilled. And in the sudden silence she was at peace. The desire which burned with so bright a flame burnt still; she wanted Crawford not one iota less; but she knew now with complete and utter certainty that neither the threat of man nor the blandishments of the devil would ever persuade her to break her vow.

Having made her decision she found, to her surprise and embarrassment, that she was crying and almost too weak to rise from her chair. And the tears were still wet on her cheeks when her husband came swinging down from the sand-dunes.

As they looked at each other it came to them both how pitiably far apart they had drifted in the last twenty-four hours. At the very moment they should have been one, they had each been walking a different trail, alone.

He sat beside her. Nervously at first and more than a little afraid that she would laugh at or not understand him, he began to tell her about the golden seal and his casually given promise to Eric. And as soon as he had finished, she in turn—nervously and more than a little afraid that he would be angry with her—told him about Crawford and how she had thought it would be fun to flirt with him and how the flirting had nearly got out of hand and then she had been sorry she had ever begun it. And although nothing much was solved and although they hit on no panacea which would rid them at one stroke of sealer and golden seal, the fact that they were at peace with themselves and each other seemed to be the only thing that mattered. For surely now they were together, now they were one, even the gates of hell could not prevail against them.

13

ON the lower slopes of Shishaldin the snow lay thick, and caribou and Kodiak bears, driven from their usual feeding grounds, padded around the mouth of the estuary. The bear with the crab-like limp hunted well that day, his hunger a thing of the past; and at nightfall he climbed the bank and lay in the shelter of the steep-sided sand-dune which overlooked Secret Water. From there he watched the golden seals. For the golden seals, his instinct told him, would soon be heading back for the sea—and the pups looked succulent as caribou calves, and a great deal easier to catch.

Normally Jim would have spent the day re-setting his traps on the fringe of the lowered snow-line. But not now. Now he stayed close to his family, awaiting the return of the sealer.

And the hours passed slowly.

In the afternoon all four of them went down to the river and re-set and strengthened the salmon baskets. The baskets didn't need re-setting or strengthening; but it helped to kill time. And it was while Jim was doubling the rope and wicker-work lashings, and playing in between times with Jess, that the idea came to him; an idea so simple that he could only wonder he hadn't thought of it before. He'd load the *Bear* with pelts and sail her to Dutch Harbour; and he'd offer the sealer a passage.

He talked over the idea with Tania. To his disappointment she was none too enthusiastic.

'Do you think he'll agree to go with you?'

His lips tightened. 'If he doesn't I'll have to persuade him.' And he nodded at the rifle stowed under the rhododendrons.

At that her eyes widened in fear.

'No. Not that. That's just what he's waiting for.'

'How do you mean, it's what he's waiting for?'

She bit her lip. 'He's a bad man. He'd think nothing of killing you.'

'Come off it, Tania!'

'But it's true. I know.' And as she saw he was by no means convinced, she added shyly, twisting and untwisting her hands, 'Don't you see, Jim, if he killed you he could have everything he wanted.'

He looked at her and understood and was appalled. A sudden anger took hold of him. This man, this sealer whose life they had saved, what was he doing to them, destroying their dreams, leading them into temptation and now it seemed threatening their very lives; and while he did all this and more, were they to sit passively by and do nothing? Yet Tania's warning had sense in it; he saw that. For several minutes he worked at the salmon traps in silence, then his mind was made up.

'All right,' his voice was final, 'if he behaves himself he can stay. But if he starts creatin' a nuisance I'll cart him back to Dutch Harbour whether he likes it or not. And'—as an afterthought—'we'll load the pelts on to the *Bear* right away. Just in case.'

They spent the rest of the afternoon loading up the furs and making an inventory . . . Kodiak bear three, arctic fox (blue) twenty-seven, silver fox four, marten eleven, mink thirty-nine, snowshoe rabbit eighty-four . . . a valuable cargo even though September was a poor month for selling.

They were lashing the last of the pelts to the yawl's deck when Crawford came plodding up-river. He had been tramping the bank for close on twelve hours; and, to judge from his ill-temper, his search had been unrewarded.

All the way back from the quicksands anger had been building up inside him: cold, calculating anger: anger that he, Howard Hamilton Crawford, was being played for a sucker. And by a polite old man and a virtuous chit of a squaw-girl!

For he was certain now that they had found and killed the gold furred seal and were hiding her pelt.

What other explanation was possible? With his own eyes, less than forty-eight hours before, he had seen the golden seal struggle ashore close to the mouth of the estuary; once ashore, he was certain she wouldn't put back to sea until the waves had dropped—for no creature could live in the gravel-shot undertow of the great combers still pounding the beach.

77

Yet he had searched the bank, the lagoons and the estuary—searched them twice with painstaking care—and she was not to be found. So they *must* have shot her and hidden her. No doubt as soon as he left the island they planned to unearth her pelt and take it to Dutch Harbour.

But he had the answer to that. He'd not leave Unimak until he had discovered where they were hiding her. And if the old man and the girl didn't fancy his staying, well that was just too bad for them.

He clumped into the *barabara*. He kicked off his boots. His oilskins he tossed to the floor, his gunbelt to the bed. No harm in making himself at home. He looked up and saw the squaw-girl watching him through the kitchen door; and as their eyes met memories of yesterday came flooding back. And with the memories, desire: desire and the urge to revenge himself, the desire to hurt and humiliate. He rolled his oilskins into a bundle. He walked slowly through to the kitchen. He tossed the bundle to Tania.

'Get these dry for me.'

Anger flared up in her, but was at once doused down; and without a word she took the oilskins into the *beleek* hut and strung them over the driftwood fire. By the time she got back Crawford had collected his boots. He kicked them towards her across the floor.

'And these.'

She hesitated, then bent down. But before she could pick them up a voice, sharp as a whip, jerked her round.

'Don't touch them, Tania.'

And she saw her husband framed in the doorway. His eyes were angry; and his hands—unbandaged now—rested on his hips close to his gunbelt.

'Leave us.' He jerked his head at the doorway.

She backed out of the room, trembling, her face white.

'Be careful!' she whispered. 'Oh, please be careful!'

Crawford moistened his lips. With his gunbelt a dozen

78

paces away, he had been caught at a disadvantage. The worm had chosen an inconvenient moment to turn.

'Seems you've forgotten your manners, mister.' Jim Lee's voice was angry.

This, Crawford decided, was no time to bring things to a head. He was conciliatory and slightly surprised.

'What's bitin' you? Only askin' to have my kit dried.'

'I don't fancy your way of asking. Now listen here. No!'— as Crawford started edging towards him—'You stay right where you are.' His hands slid meaningly to his belt. 'You listen, and don't interrupt. Ever since you come to this island you've been makin' mischief. You start totin' a gun, you start prowlin' about in the middle of the night, you start makin' calf's eyes at my wife, and now you start throwin' your weight around. Well mister, this time you've gone a step too far. Tomorrow I'm takin' you back to Dutch Harbour.' A pause while this sank in, then, 'My boat's down there on the beach all loaded up. I'm sailing tomorrow at sunrise, seven o'clock sharp. And you're coming with me.'

'And if I choose not to?'

The revolver was in Jim's hand now. He patted it.

'You'll come.'

Crawford was half angry, half relieved. Angry to be lectured like a child, relieved to find that the issue between them was not being brought to a head on the spot.

'You finished your sermon?'

'I've quit talking. But you stay right there awhile.'

He sidled past the sealer, picked the gunbelt off the bed and transferred the ·45 Webley from Crawford's holster to his own.

'Think I'll keep this. Jest till we get to Dutch Harbour.'

Then he was gone and Crawford was left alone, angry and slightly incredulous.

You fool, he thought; you simple-minded old fool. If you

had to pick a quarrel, why didn't you see it through while you held the cards? You won't be so lucky next time. You don't really imagine, do you, that come sun-up I'll be trotting down to your boat like a dog to its master's whistle?

SOMETHING was going on. Eric was certain of it. Something exciting.

He could tell in a dozen ways. His mother and father whispering together and stopping and suddenly doing things the moment they saw him; Uncle Howard poking about in father's gunrack and pulling a long face when he found all the rifles had gone; and the *Bear* down at the water's edge and loaded with pelts—though everyone knew that September was a bad month for selling.

And the trouble was that all too soon it would be bedtime and he'd be banished to the bunk above Jess's where he'd be left out of things and would miss all the fun—whatever the fun was going to be.

'Eric!'

To his great relief it wasn't his father looking at his watch and pointing to the *barabara*; it was Uncle Howard.

'Yes, Uncle Howard?'

'You like to play a game?'

'Oh yes!' This was at least a reprieve. 'What are we going to play?'

'You like a ride on my back? Like a cowboy at a rodeo?'

Well, it wasn't what *he* would have chosen—rather childish really, more like the sort of game his mother played with Jess —but he thought it would be impolite to say so. Gravely he clambered on to the sealer's back.

The game exceeded his expectations. Uncle Howard proved a fierce and very active horse. He bucked and jigged and skittered this way and that like a snowshoe rabbit chased by a fox, Eric clinging to his neck. And when at last with much puffing and snorting he sank to the ground, the little boy—still triumphantly astride him—was eager for more.

'Another ride, Uncle Howard. Just one more. Please.'

At that moment Jim Lee came round the side of the *barabara*. He pulled up short.

'Eric!' His voice was sharp. 'Bedtime.'

'Oh Dad! We're havin' a wonderful game. Just a few more minutes. Please!'

Jim was uncertain. Get him away from the sealer, his instinct warned him. And yet he wanted to be fair. It could be that Crawford was making an effort to be friendly; what harm could the boy come to by playing with him (especially as he and Tania were within earshot), and hadn't he enough on his plate without further alienating the sealer—not to mention his son?

'All right then. But ten minutes only. Then you got to come in.'

Crawford looked up. 'I'll send him in, mister.'

'Thanks.'

He walked back to the *barabara*. He didn't know why his suspicions were still unsloughed. But they were. He shut the door. He dropped to his hands and knees and crawled to the window. He crouched under the sill, listening. His son's voice came to him muffled and distorted, but quite understandable.

'You be my horse again.'

'Just once. Then we play a quieter game. I'm fair whacked!'

It sounded harmless enough. But before Jim went back to the kitchen, just as a precaution, he opened windows and door—so that any sort of an altercation he'd hear . . .

The second ride was as good as the first with many a buck and rear and sideways jig; but at last Eric was dislodged. Hopefully he clung to the sealer's leg.

'How 'bout one more!'

Crawford shook his head. 'You sit nice an' quiet a while. Right 'longside me. I got something to tell you.'

'A story?'

'Well, I guess you might call it a sort of a story.' He waited till the little boy was settled. Then, suddenly serious, 'You remember the first time we met, Eric? Down by the river?'

The boy nodded.

'An' you remember tellin' me you found something during the storm? Something real special. And I could have three guesses what it was?'

'Sure. I remember.'

'Well, now didn't I have only two guesses down by the river? Then I lumped you across.'

The little boy, puzzled, nodded. 'That's right, mister.'

'Well,' Crawford smiled, 'ever since lumpin' you across the river I been thinkin' about my last guess. An' now I'm ready to make it.'

'Ooooh! What you going to guess? I bet you don't guess right!'

Crawford put his hands over his eyes. He began to rock to and fro. 'I got to work myself into a sorta trance,' he explained to Eric; 'that way I can see what you were up to during the storm.'

And Jim Lee, looking out of the window, was reassured. There was after all nothing ominous about the sudden silence. It was just that they were playing a quieter game, some sort of sitting-down blind-man's-buff.

Crawford swayed to and fro. His voice took on the sing-song cadence of a man in a trance. 'I can see it all.' A pause. 'I can see it like in a dream. You an' a great big furry animal lyin' side by side . . .'

'You're warm! You're real warm!'

'An' she's a wonderful glowin' yellow, like the sun. An' she's got babies with her. One, is it? Or two? Or three?'

The little boy hopped up and down in delight.

'She sure got two babies. But what *is* she?'

'I can see now'—triumphantly—'she's a golden seal.'

'Ooooh! I never thought you'd guess!'

So, by God, he'd been right! But what had they done with her? Between his fingers his eyes slid round at the boy. An arm twisted behind his back and he'd soon tell. But it was risky, so close to his parents. He'd try it the easy way first.

'Eric! Where is she?'

The little boy was silent. He had remembered his father's warning.

'Where is she, Eric?'

'I dunno.'

'You don't know! But didn't you help your Dad carry away her pelt?'

'Her pelt! But she's not dead, mister!'

'You mean your Dad didn't shoot her?' He was incredulous.

'No'—proudly—'I made him promise me *not* to shoot her. 'Cause she's my friend, see.'

A pause, a long disbelieving pause. Then, 'Let's get this straight now. You say you found this golden seal, an' you told your father where she was on the understandin' he wouldn't shoot her?'

'That's right.'

'Well now, if *I* promise you not to shoot her, will you tell *me* where she is?'

Eric was uncertain. 'What you wanta know where she is for?'

The sealer smiled, a practised easy smile. 'Tell you the truth I've been wantin' to see a golden seal for years. I've heard they're real pretty. But I never been able to find one.'

'You mean'—doubtfully—'you just want to look at her?'

'Sure.'

'And if I tell you where she is you'll promise me never to hurt her? Or her babies?'

'Sure I'll promise.'

'All right then. Cross your heart an' say after me, 'I promise never, never, never to hurt the golden seal. God strike me dead if I break my promise.'

He didn't hesitate. He crossed his heart. He repeated the childish, meaningless words. Why not? It was only a little boy's game.

And when he had made his promise Eric took him by the hand and led him a few yards up the sand-dune and showed him the way to Secret Water.

15

IT was only after two hours' surreptitious poking and prying that he found one of the rifles, wedged into the roof of the *beleek* hut. He took it and buried it secretly in the sand a little way from the *barabara*. And then he was happy, knowing that once again things were panning out well: that once again he was going to get what he wanted. He made his preparations with care, and soon only one thing remained to be done before the stage was set for the grand finale; he had to speak to the squaw-girl alone.

His opportunity came a little before dark when the scar-faced man went off to the *beleek* hut to bank down the fire for the night.

The moment Jim Lee had left the room and he and the girl were alone tension welled up, quickly and frighteningly, like water rising in a ship's compartment that has been stove in by the sea. Tania's hand slid to the comforting bulge of her revolver.

'Don't try anything.' Her voice was breathless. 'I mightn't miss a second time.'

That did it: rubbing salt into his wounded vanity. Any compunction he might have felt for her, any scruples about what he was going to do were drowned in anger now.

'Listen, Tania.' His voice was malicious. 'I've got your gold furred seal—if you don't believe me go look in Secret Water. And I've got your guns—if you don't believe me go look in the roof o' the *beleek* hut. So *I'm* the one who's holdin' the cards. An' *I'm* the one who's callin' the tune.'

She stared at him in horror, her dreams shattered, her hopes trampled to dust and the fears she had believed to be things of the past once again crowding in on her. And the voice of the sealer went on, venomous and evil.

'Now listen. An' don't interrupt. If I say I won't go to Dutch Harbour your husband will try and take me by force, won't he? An' if he does that I swear by God I'll kill him.' A pause. 'Have you ever seen a man shot in the stomach, Tania? It isn't a pretty sight. Sometimes a man who's been shot in the stomach lives for days.'

She covered her face. She rocked to and fro. 'But why? Why? What have we done to you? Oh, why can't you leave us alone?'

'I might be persuaded to.'

She looked at him, uncomprehending.

'A pretty girl like you could persuade a man to do a lot of things.'

She still didn't get it. And in her distress she failed to notice that he was edging imperceptibly closer.

'Looks like I have to give it you in words of one syllable.' He smiled at her. 'I promised myself two things before I left Unimak. The golden seal and you. When I've got what I want, I'll go. Not before.'

He was prepared for what happened next. He saw understanding and then anger, blind uncontrollable anger, rise up in her; he saw the downward flick of her eyes, the hand edging towards the gun. Before it was out of her pocket he was across the room. His hand chopped down on her wrist. The gun fell to the floor. He picked it up.

'One o'clock tonight,' he said quietly, 'and you come to the sandhill next to Secret Water. You come alone, and you leave your guns and your knives behind. Else, by God I'll kill you as well as your husband.'

She backed against the wall. Her tongue ran over her lips.

The dart of the tongue fascinated him; the dart of the tongue and the frightened eyes and the moistening of the lips which he knew, given half a chance, could be passionate. He jerked her towards him, and for the second time in forty-eight hours his mouth reached for hers. She neither resisted nor responded. She simply let him kiss her, as though the mouth his lips were pressed to belonged to a stranger whose affairs were of complete indifference to her. Angrily he pushed her away.

'Go on,' his voice was contemptuous, 'scream! Why don't you scream for your kind old husband to come and protect you?'

She turned. Blindly. Knocking into tables and chairs, she blundered out of the room.

16

HE moved fast. Before the sound of her blundering footsteps had died away, he was out of the *barabara*. A crouching zigzagging run to the dip in the bank and he was out of sight; a scrabbling burrow in the sand and he had unearthed the rifle. Then in the gathering darkness he ran down-dune to the water's edge. Panting, he crouched beneath the keel of the *Bear*.

It was a good position, affording cover, shelter and a first-class view. He looked up-river to where the *barabara* stood silhouetted against the skyline. Anyone leaving it could be seen, could be picked off. He checked the rifle, rubbing it free from sand and slipping the safety catch.

Not that he expected to use the rifle. According to his reckoning there would be no one leaving the *barabara* until midnight—for the girl would be too afraid of her husband getting a bullet in him to talk. He smiled. How well everything was turning out! How foolish they had been to cross swords with him! Hadn't he warned the girl that he always got his way in the end: that, like the restless sea on which he had spent his life, what he wanted he took?

The hours passed and the lights went out in the *barabara* and everything was very still and very quiet.

He looked at his watch; coming up to eleven o'clock. He looked at the sky, never at this time of year completely dark and shot now with the silver of a rising moon. He looked at the waves, ironing out to a comfortable swell—so once he got back he'd have no difficulty in launching the yawl by himself. He checked his equipment: rifle, revolver, knife, rope (for hauling back the pelt) and food (which he cached in the yawl for his return). He had already decided on his route, along a corridor of shadow where sand-dunes blocked off the light of the low-slung moon and where little patches of pre-dawn mist were already beginning to form. Quietly he rose to his feet. Quietly, at a wary well-oiled lope, he set out for Secret Water.

He crawled past the pool then doubled back and came up to it stealthily from the landward—he was almost certain the man and his squaw-girl were still in the *barabara*, but there was no harm in taking precautions. Everything was as he expected. There was no ambush. Only 'she with the yellow hair', her fur ablaze in the moonlight like the gold of the mythical fleece. She was restive, zigzagging the pool in sudden darts, her pups strung out in her wake. Another couple of hours, he thought, and she might well have been putting to sea. But she was too late now.

He unslung his rifle. He balanced carefully on one knee. His sights steadied between the golden seal's eyes. And then he heard, unexpectedly, the voice of the little boy, 'Say after me, I promise never, never, never to hurt the golden seal.' The sights of his rifle wavered, and he cursed. He must be getting soft. What man in his right mind wouldn't break a carelessly given promise for the sake of 2,000 dollars? He raised his rifle again.

Behind him a stone glissaded down the reverse slope of the bank. He jerked round, obsessed by a sudden fear. But it was only a gull which rose with a rustle of wings from the crest of the sand-dunes; for a second its silhouette was outlined against the disc of the moon, then it was gone and the bank once again lay still and silent under the stars. Howard Hamilton Crawford, he chided himself, you're nervous as an old woman; pull yourself together. He raised his rifle for the third time. Third time lucky, he thought; nothing's

going to stop me this time. His rifle steadied. His trigger-finger tightened.

He had no presentiment of fear and no premonition of retribution. Why should he have? Wasn't everything going according to plan? He didn't see the mass of ebony, darker than even the darkness around it, rise up behind him. He didn't hear the pad of the great steel-tipped paws as the bear came out from the shadow of the steep-sided sand-dune. The first thing he heard was the cough, the sharp excited cough of a Kodiak about to kill.

He spun round, his finger snatching involuntarily at the trigger and the bullet parting the fur on the golden seal's back and ricocheting off the rocks on the farther side of the pool. And the bear was on him.

He screamed. He swung up his rifle and fired, but the bullet, six inches too high, glanced off the bone of the Kodiak's forehead. He saw the silvered claws swing back for the kill. He saw the great mouth, tooth-stumped and salivared, open wide. But he didn't hear the angry roar which echoed his requiem among the sandhills. He heard only the voice of a child: shrieking, again and again, 'God strike me dead if I break my promise. God strike me dead if I break my promise.' He flung up the rifle to guard his face. But the powerful paws smashed through barrel and stock and ripped the flesh off his arm from elbow to wrist. Most men would have died of shock. But Crawford wasn't the sort to die easily. He jerked out his knife. He ducked under the flailing paws and left-handed stabbed the bear to the heart.

The Kodiak swayed on his feet. His eyes glazed. But his claws still flayed at the sealer's back, tearing off great ribbons of muscle and flesh, cracking and splintering bone. And the life-blood poured out of Howard Hamilton Crawford, turning the gold of the sand to red.

And all the while, as the waves of pain surged up and up to crash unendurably loud in Crawford's brain, the voice of the little boy went on screaming louder and louder, shriller and shriller: 'God strike me dead if I break my promise.' It was the last thing he heard before his spine snapped like the back of a grounded ship and he heard no more for ever.

The bear swayed. His paws tore at the haft of the knife; but it was lodged too firm and too deep. Blood thickened in his throat. He fell. His eyes rolled sightlessly at the moon, and in the shade of the sandhill the only living things were the frightlessly sleeping gulls.

17

THEY lay side by side, the Kodiak bear and the sealer, the frost on their bodies melting fast in the warmth of the rising sun and above them the sea-gulls gathering. It was the gulls which led Jim and Tania to them.

In the pale half-light of dawn he dropped to his knees beside them, listening, wondering. Then he closed Crawford's eyes. Tania watched him.

'Are they both dead?'

He nodded. 'It's all over, Tania.'

An hour later they were burying Crawford on the lower

slopes of Shishaldin at a spot where the mountain's knees fell sheer to the marshland beneath, a spot too barren to be hunted over and too remote to be visited by chance. They buried him deep in the gravelly earth. They piled heavy stones over his grave—for the Kodiak bears are inquisitive grubbers. And it seemed to Tania a terrible thing that there should be no tears, no sighs and no lamentations; only a feeling of God-sent relief (as might be felt by those aboard a ship which has near foundered in a tempest but has struggled at last into a haven both safe and familiar). And soon the burial was over and done with and they were walking back towards Secret Water.

'Jim.' Tania's voice was anxious.

'Hmmm?'

'You reckon he killed the golden seal?'

He shook his head. 'If he'd killed her we'd have found her body.'

'You reckon she's still on the island then?' Her eyes were troubled.

He knew what she was thinking: that so long as the golden seal remained on Unimak she would be a reminder of things best forgotten, a perpetuator of doubts, temptations and fear. He was wondering how he could reassure her when a glint of gold a little way down the bank caught his eye.

'Look, Tania.'

They stood close together, watching, as she with the yellow hair led her pups back to the safety of the world she knew and was safe in—the open sea. The golden seals moved in single file, slipping and slithering awkwardly on the loose-packed stones, wheeled over by puzzled echelons of gulls. At the water's edge they didn't pause. They plunged straight in. And in a moment they were transformed into creatures of grace. Gone was their awkwardness; even the new-born pups rode the rollers with instinctive ease. Soon the tide rip had caught them and was whirling them out through the

sand-bars, out to the world they belonged to—the lonely reaches of the Pacific.

Jim Lee stared after them long past the time they were out of sight.

'Do you mind very much?'—Tania's voice came to him as if from far away.

'No,' he said.

He said it automatically, to comfort her. It wasn't until the word was spoken that he realized it was true. In his heart he had expected to feel a twinge of disappointment when the gold furred seal was put, finally and irrevocably, beyond his reach—for he knew that dreams die hard. And yet now she was gone he felt only relief. My dream wasn't much of a dream, was it, he thought. And anyhow what do I want with dreams when I've so much else beside?

'No,' he said, 'I don't mind at all. In fact I'm glad she's gone.'

She smiled at him. She moved the tips of her fingers, very gently, over his face. 'I'm glad you're glad,' she said.

As they headed back for the *barabara* the mist lifted clear of the hills and a rainbow, peacock-hued, spanned the sky between heaven and earth. Soon they came to the river. They forded it hand in hand, watched by the ever-circling gulls and by three little Kodiak bears fishing in waters crystal clear and beautiful as that other river which ran out, long ago, from another Eden.

All these books are available at your local bookshop or newsagent, or can be ordered direct from the publisher.

To order direct from the publisher just tick the titles you want and fill in the form below.

Name _____

Address _____

Send to:
Dragon Cash Sales
PO Box 11, Falmouth, Cornwall TR10 9EN.

Please enclose remittance to the value of the cover price plus:

UK 45p for the first book, 20p for the second book plus 14p per copy for each additional book ordered to a maximum charge of £1.63.

BFPO and Eire 45p for the first book, 20p for the second book plus 14p per copy for the next 7 books, thereafter 8p per book.

Overseas 75p for the first book and 21p for each additional book.